Eleanor,

TREASURE ISLAND SEAL

Sunset SEALs Book 3

SHARON HAMILTON

Congrats! Enjoy Ned & Madison's Story!

♡ Sharon Hamilton

SHARON HAMILTON'S BOOK LIST

SEAL BROTHERHOOD BOOKS

SEAL BROTHERHOOD SERIES

Accidental SEAL Book 1

Fallen SEAL Legacy Book 2

SEAL Under Covers Book 3

SEAL The Deal Book 4

Cruisin' For A SEAL Book 5

SEAL My Destiny Book 6

SEAL of My Heart Book 7

Fredo's Dream Book 8

SEAL My Love Book 9

SEAL Encounter Prequel to Book 1

SEAL Endeavor Prequel to Book 2

Ultimate SEAL Collection Vol. 1 Books 1-4 /2 Prequels

Ultimate SEAL Collection Vol. 2 Books 5-7

BAD BOYS OF SEAL TEAM 3 SERIES

SEAL's Promise Book 1

SEAL My Home Book 2

SEAL's Code Book 3

Big Bad Boys Bundle Books 1-3

BAND OF BACHELORS SERIES

Lucas Book 1

All of Sharon's books are available on Audible,
narrated by the talented J.D. Hart.

ABOUT THE BOOK

Navy SEAL Ned Silver is lured to the Florida gulf coast by the friend of his fathers, a former Navy diver now turned treasure hunter. Between deployments, S.O. Silver is addicted to adventure, and searching for pirate booty is right up his alley. What he hasn't counted on is that his net has also captured a local mermaid.

Madison Montgomery has done freelance underwater modeling and film work, but she's also an experienced scuba diver. Between jobs, she tends a salty beach bar catering to whatever the sea blows in. She's unprepared when her heart is hooked on the muscled beach bum she's hired to work with on a treasure dive.

As their underwater love affair smolders like a hyperbaric welding torch, the pair will have to discover who is captain and who is captured.

AUTHOR'S NOTE

When I was researching some of the treasure hunting and shipwreck stories, I came across the story about a barge that used to run a regular route between Cuba, the Tampa Bay area, and sometimes further North. This barge sank, and just like in my story, only three crew members survived.

There also was a cook on this barge, and he always traveled with a dog who was said to be the good luck charm of the crew. The three surviving members last vision of the barge, as it was sinking, was seeing the cook, swimming for shore. Right behind him was his little dog.

I like to think the two of them somehow survived, though the odds were probably not great, since it was said no one else did. But who knows? Perhaps they lived on. Perhaps the dog had puppies of his own. And maybe one of them, decades later, became a stray on the beach at Treasure Island.

I go to bed thinking about that, and it makes me smile. I hope you enjoy this story about a man re-connecting with the past of his father, seeking adventure and finding the real treasure of his life, his mermaid, Madison.

Maybe Ned pens this poem in a future story:

Madison

A warm-bodied vision of perfection, she comes to me
as I sleep

Timid and frolicking in the turquoise waters of her
world

Timeless and free of the trappings of mine.

She knows I'm watching her

Just by the way she waves, by the way her body
undulates to the gentle current

Flying in the bright blue fresh air of the ocean

Her touch is light as if not to disturb

But everlasting and unforgettable.

She is everything I am not.

And she is everything I need.

Sharon Hamilton
April, 2020

I support two main charities. Navy SEAL/UDT Museum operates in Ft. Pierce, Florida. Please learn about this wonderful museum, all run by active and former SEALs and their friends and families, and who rely on public support, not that of the U.S. Government. www.navysealmuseum.org

IF YOU GOT ANY CLOSER, YOU WOULD HAVE TO ENLIST

I also support Wounded Warriors, who tirelessly bring together the warrior as well as the family members who are just learning to deal with their soldier's condition and have nowhere to turn. It is a long path to becoming well, but I've seen first-hand what this organization does for its warriors and the families who love them. Please give what your heart tells you is right. If you cannot give, volunteer at one of the many service centers all over the United States. Get involved. Do something meaningful for someone who gave so much of themselves, to families who have paid the price for your freedom. You'll find a family there unlike any other on the planet.

www.woundedwarriorproject.org

CHAPTER 1

NAVY SEAL NED Silver fingered the pendant his father had left him. He should have been happy to receive such a gift—this "piece of eight" treasure mounted in a sterling silver setting adorned by a voluptuous mermaid. His dad wore it just about twenty-four seven. He'd whispered to Ned when he was little that the mermaid had been his secret love, number two to Ned's mother, of course. Something about that story pissed him off every time he recalled it.

"He wanted you to have it, Ned," his mother whispered, pressing the piece into his palm and then curling his fingers around it.

"I always pictured him taking it to his grave." He let the curves of the mermaid glisten in the sun, the tail slowly moving back and forth as he fluttered his fingers underneath her. He'd touched it only once over the years, when he'd found it on his dad's dresser. It called to him.

"No, he never wanted that for her," his mother said casually. "It would be like burying her alive all over again. At least, that's what I think your father would say."

She was referring to the fact that the coin pendant had been plucked from the warm waters of the Florida Keys by the "Pirate" Jake Silver himself more than thirty years ago, on a pleasure dive with his best friend. Back when his dad was healthy. A risk-taker. Just after Ned was conceived and during what his mother called a "rough patch".

He caressed the shapely form of the mermaid with his thumb, fondling her with respect. It was a symbol that the torch had been passed. Ned would be his own man now, regardless that he'd become one of America's elite warriors a decade ago, a member of Seal Team 3 out of Coronado.

She belongs in the ocean anyway, never to be buried on land, he heard his father say.

At least some of his dad's tall tales had taken hold. He remembered them more and more as the days passed since his father's hospital confinement and ultimate death. It was funny how that worked, he thought. The long good-bye brought back into focus all the stories and memories they'd shared over his lifetime. Bringing back that which was lost. Memories buried and now unearthed. Strangely, this gift symbolized the last handshake between father and son, a compass to point the way to Ned's future. A portent of what was to come.

His mother used to laugh a lot more before his dad got sick. Old Pirate Jake drank like a fish until the very end, often didn't come home and never called her, either. She loved the bastard and welcomed him back every time. She was the backbone of this family, and her love was strong enough to keep them all together when money was tight and Ned scented fear in the household.

Even from a young age, Ned could smell fear around him. It was a constant friend, even though a pesky one.

Today, after the funeral, his mother looked tired and cried-out, her lips forming a thin straight line as if they'd never shared a smile between them or had ever mated. She was stern but unflappable. Her worry lines were deeper despite the makeup she'd recently started to wear.

His father had taken a long time to die, and he took a piece of her with him to his grave.

"Thanks, Mom," he said as he felt her body melt into him when he hugged her. He vowed to spend more time with her because of the void left with his dad's passing. He sensed her vulnerability and fragility. The hero in him grew taller and his chest sprang out.

He knew he couldn't right every wrong or save everyone on the planet, but it didn't stop him from trying.

She wiped her cheeks and plastered a brave grin to her face without changing the vacancy in her eyes.

It scared him when he realized that now more than ever before, it was important that he remain safe and always return home from deployments and dangerous trainings—*for her,* since there wasn't another woman in his life. She wouldn't be able to handle that on top of his father's passing. She loved him with everything she had. He loved the mermaid and the promise of adventure.

Ned slipped the mermaid around his neck like a tiny silver anchor.

"It suits you."

In truth, he'd always thought it was gaudy, that his dad had been showing off. But her face brightened, and that was worth everything. Afterall, it was just a trinket that lay buried for nearly four hundred years until the Pirate stole her away from Davy Jones himself, claiming her for his own. He could do that. He could watch over both his father's women.

His mother's half-sister, Aunt Flo, the one everyone worried about, approached and hugged them both.

"So good we could all be together, isn't it?"

She realized her words fell flat.

"Well, all except for—" She stopped herself and

then redirected, something she'd learned to do in numerous therapy sessions and hospitalizations. "Well, we should all do something like go to a movie!"

That fell even flatter. Ned didn't have words, but his mother did, ever the gracious one in the family, regardless of how she was treated.

"Flo, I know what you meant," his mother said as she extricated herself from the bear-hug. She was covering for his poor aunt, just like she did when she paid for the items Flo had stolen from the dime store and insisted she'd bought with her own money. She had a full drawer of lipsticks she never wore and owned more socks, still in their wrappers, than she owned underwear. She was a compulsive gambler, too, with a terrible memory of what she'd spent. The wheels were beginning to fall off the cart more and more every day.

Ned needed a break. Growing up, he thought she was funny and couldn't understand why his father got so upset being around her. Now he understood. Now he could get away from her.

Ned gave his aunt a peck on the cheek and headed toward a small group of friends from high school who had come to the memorial. They were signing the guest book and placing a picture on the poster.

"Hey, Carson, thanks for coming, man."

Tanned and looking like a professional surfer, his best buddy on the swim and basketball teams in high school showed off his pearly whites. "No problem. I found this nice one here of you and me and your dad. Thought maybe your mom would like having it around."

Ned eyed the small photograph with him and Carson in their Cubs Little League uniforms, his dad playing coach. Coach Silver had insisted on grabbing the number one for himself, which Ned had forgotten, and it made him chuckle.

"What a couple of skinny kids we were then," Ned whispered. After some thought, he added, "What were we, ten?"

"Just about," said Carson, his arm around the shoulder of a pretty girl, also from their school. *Jackie*, he thought. Ned couldn't remember her last name and wasn't sure she was actually in their class or the one below.

"Jackie? That you?"

He'd always had a major crush on her, but Jackie hadn't given him the time of day. Now it was completely different, and the roles were reversed. She'd grown up nice, and it appeared to be her turn to want to make an impression.

"Ned. I'm so sorry," she said timidly.

He accepted her floral-scented embrace and noted Carson's worry line form at the top of his nose, so he kept their hug brief. He scrambled to fill the air with something else.

"So you guys seeing each other now or what?"

"Gawd, Ned, we're married five years now, have one kid and another one we're working on."

Although Carson was casual, Jackie blushed. Ned couldn't help but look at her belly and then cursed himself and glanced away.

"I'm sorry. I've not been around much, and I've lost track of time and all my friends." It was all he could think of, and it was a dumb-ass excuse at that.

"Oh, shut up. You were off being a hero while the rest of us went to college and started families. I can't believe you aren't married yet, you stud."

Ned had always been uneasy with the reputation he had as a great lover of women when, in fact, he had little experience. Most people would be surprised to learn he couldn't remember his last sexual encounter. He loved women, but he didn't like the drama he saw between the sexes, and he never liked hooking up with damaged goods. He stuck to what he was best at— *saving the day*. If women didn't come running after him, then he wasn't going to run after them, either. Time appeared to have slipped away while he was off being a hero.

He shrugged.

"A Navy SEAL. That's so impressive," Jackie gushed, batting her eyes. "Your dad must have been proud."

That one hurt. Good old Pirate Jake was long in the stories but short in the ways he showed his pride or affection. Growing up, Ned had taken it to mean his dad wanted him to be a man's man. Now, at thirty-one, he figured most men-women relationships caused more scars than bridges or healthy connections. He saw more anchors than golden magical bonds. Maybe he really was in love with mermaids, who floated around in the light blue waters of their own world, skimpily clad and elusive. Beautiful to watch but impossible to love.

So he decided to tell the truth because his dad wasn't there to smack him.

"To be honest, Carson, I think my dad would have preferred I go to college like you and become a tax attorney."

The couple gave him long looks, blinking slowly.

"Just kidding." He glanced down at the picture again and saw the gold and silver mermaid pendant around his dad's neck. Even as the team coach, he was still showing off. His life was bigger than his death, and there wasn't a chance he'd ever be forgotten.

CHAPTER 2

MADISON MONTGOMERY EYED the group of silver-haired bikers who had blasted their way into the Salty Dog. Iris picked up her order tray and rounded the bar until Madison grabbed her by the arm.

"Hold it there. These guys might mean trouble. I'm going to take them. Sorry."

Iris pouted. "I can handle them."

Madison towered over the part-time college kid by four inches. From a wealthy Northeastern family, Iris embodied an ingenue having her fling in Florida's gulf coast. Madison dropped the rag she'd been using to wipe the wooden plank bar and brushed her waist-length blonde hair, including one errant curl over her forehead, back behind her then looked down at the young woman in a death stare.

"That's exactly what I'm afraid of. You get the next one, but watch the bar for me."

It didn't matter what Iris was going to say. Madison

was three feet away already.

She had a habit of not looking too closely at the rough crowd and never making eye contact until she'd spoken. She didn't care what they were thinking coming in as long as they were on her side by the time she finished her speech.

They were a collection of misfits, covered in tats and torn jeans, revealing oversized hairy legs. One was wearing the bottom half of a green leisure suit with a yellow stripe down the side. That's when she knew they weren't badasses at all but posers. They could wear all the bandanas, leather jackets and earrings they wanted, but she wasn't fooled and knew she could mess with them. They were probably accountants trying to play like the Sons of Anarchy. The one with the black eyepatch spoke to her first.

"Madison, dearie. How's it going, sweetheart?"

She recognized him immediately. He was the owner of the *Barry Bones* dive boat and sometimes treasure scavenger, except his name was Noonan. He was an occasional friend but mostly a past boyfriend of her mother's. Growing up, Madison even wondered if he was her father, until she was introduced to him years later. She knew it needled him that she'd thought that way about him so decided to pour it on a bit more than usual.

"Hey, Dad, you're looking pretty poor." She pointed to his lower thigh, indicating the whiteness she witnessed. "You need a little more beach time and less time on the gulf."

"Ahhh, don't ruin my reputation. If I'd have knocked up someone so fine as your mother, I would have tied her up and kidnapped her until she'd put a ring on it. Never happened. You know that. Not that I didn't try."

The statement was meant for his buddies, not really for Madison's ears.

That got a rousing series of shouts from the table and demands for three pitchers of beer, the cheapest way to go. Older, divorced men like this were, for the most part, penniless, and sharing apartments or sleeping on the beach. It was easier to forget to leave a tip if they ordered this way, always with the chance that someone *else* would pay the bill.

Iris was giving her the cold shoulder—even colder than usual. It was amazing how younger women were brought up these days, especially the ones who had been pampered by parents who were basically buying them off with expensive toys and vacations so they could get away from their own kids. Of course, many of the younger crowd had never had to fully provide for themselves. They didn't depend on being nice, so they weren't. It was a shame.

Madison placed the plastic pitchers under three of

the taps, turning them on to load side by side. Iris interrupted one to fill three glasses and then returned the pitcher but left the tap off. She wasn't going to give the younger woman the satisfaction of seeing a ripple in her calm ocean demeanor.

The pitchers were delivered along with five glasses. "I'm going to see if the cook has some extras he can throw in. Be right back," she said and turned before the crew could respond. She headed to scrounge some freebies from the kitchen. Even that wouldn't generate a tip.

The Salty Dog's huge Louisiana Cajun cook was ordering young Latino boys around the kitchen like the place was on fire. It smelled like it, too, and there was more smoke than usual.

"You got anything I can give to some penniless seniors, Washington?"

"Oh, I gots oysters. Up until five minutes ago, they was barbecued perfect. But now they's smoked real good. They still look pretty, though," he said, pointing a large stainless steel spatula at a plated dozen oysters covered in red sauce, sitting under a heat lamp.

"I'm taking them, Mr. Jones."

"You do that missy. You do that," he said to her back. As she slipped through the doorway, she grabbed a bag of dinner rolls.

Madison could tell her ass was being checked out

like she had eyes sewn into her rear jeans pockets. It came with the territory. If she'd wanted a "safe" job, she could have worked in a Real Estate office. But then, she'd have to contend with the possibility she'd die of boredom or fall asleep driving on the way home from the office. This worked fine and paid well, and her boss never came. It was just a temporary duty until the next underwater film or salvage dive job.

"Here you go, boys. Bread's on its way," she said as she downloaded the oysters onto her group's table without sliding them into their laps. The scramble to grab an oyster or two was messy and a little ugly. She added the rolls to a red plastic basket and dropped it off too. "That's to mop up the butter."

As the evening wore on the crowd got younger until all the "normal" people—the ones with jobs or ones who cared about their jobs—went home. In between was a smattering of older retirees. If they had money, they were in pairs. If not, they were men drinking by themselves, fantasizing on being able to bag a younger woman who might be drunk enough and wouldn't look too closely at his teeth, the grey he was covering up, or the gut he'd lovingly grown over the years.

She rarely saw a real silver fox, but those were the kind of experienced men who could satisfy her and turn her bones to butter. Men her own age were practically in diapers. She preferred the imperfect older men with tats, stories of ups and downs without regrets, and sexual experience. She liked making them feel loved. She was good at that.

Noonan himself had tried to fix her up with some of his friends, but she turned them all down before a coffee date. She was picky. She wanted a date to know exactly what to do and to be a real man, not some pretend postage stamp on a love letter. Settling down would be as difficult as bottling the ocean. It was unnatural, and except for various economic reasons, there was little reason to go there.

Being free was where it was at. At just under thirty, Madison didn't care about aging. She cared about losing her freedom.

She checked the time and discovered it was nearly midnight. Her mother would be stopping by to make her nightly visit.

Noonan LaFontaine's eye was bloodshot as he approached the bar, barely able to walk without tilting. His buddies had been long gone.

"Hold on there, Skipper. Tell your brain you're on land," she said to him and laughed at his delayed expression. Leaning into the countertop, she added, "Hope you'll let me call you a cab."

He nodded, but before she got out her cell, he grabbed her wrist. "I was lookin' for your mama, little one."

"Haven't seen her. Should be any time now."

Noonan craned his neck, checking out the outdoor restaurant, then scanned up and down the u-shaped bar and the clusters of tables along the walls. He shrugged. "The heart's willing but the body, it just won't cooperate."

She was touched Noonan wanted to see her mother. She'd been turning him down for the last twenty years, as Madison could recall. But their chemistry was something special and her mother looked younger and happier whenever the old salty captain was around.

Every woman wants to be some man's fantasy.

"I can give her a message, if you like," Madison said, placing her cell to her ear.

He waited until the cab was ordered before he answered her. "Tell her someone special has passed into the locker. I think she'll know who that is."

"Cryptic!" she said, wrinkling her brow.

"Secret!" His eyes got wide and he was a man of thirty again. Madison had asked about their relationship so many times just the mere mention of his name gave her the stop motion with the palm of her mother's hand before she could utter another syllable.

"Noonan, I'm sorry that I bug you about being my dad."

"It's okay. I guess I'm a little flattered. I still dream about what it would be like if she could ever get that heartache out of her system."

"My dad?"

"Not him. She never loved him. It was someone else."

Madison frowned, even though she knew it was true. Her mother had been fairly honest about the things she did tell her. It was all the things she didn't tell her that gave her worry.

"So this—"

Noonan cut her off by putting his forefinger to his mouth and whispering, "Shh."

She saw the soft underside of a very lonely man.

"You got any gigs I can join? Anything at all coming up?"

"We got a little contract to do a salvage, but they're looking for something specific, not looking to raze the ship. When I'm sober, I'll tell you about it. Maybe I could hire you for two, three days. We aren't quite sure the coordinates yet. Depending on the water depth, I might say no."

"How about an underwater porn film about a mermaid and a handsome seaman?"

"You okay with exposing yourself to millions of eyes?"

"Mermaids don't have anything down below that isn't naturally covered up, you know. And as for showing my tits, well, I practically do that every day wearing these tee-shirts." She held back the shoulders of her white Salty Dog shirt and showed how it stretched.

"Always a ham. You just like the attention, Madison. Always did. You're just like your mama. Just as pretty too. She broke men's hearts everywhere she went. Everywhere…"—he started, spreading his arms out wide to the sides—"everywhere she went, there was always lots of blood and bleeding. Near suicides. Your mother was an addiction, someone impossible to get out of anyone's system." He leaned closer to her. "Don't you do that with your life. Bestow your womanly wiles on some nice young man and make him the king of your kingdom and you'll live that fantasy your mother never found."

Madison straightened up. She was almost going to cry and that never happened.

Noonan put his finger to his lips. "Don't you tell her. Just tell her someone special is passed on and I wanted her to know about it."

Noonan made his way outside, got in the cab, and left safely. Madison spent the rest of the evening looking for her mother as every new face came through the entrance.

But her mother never showed.

CHAPTER 3

NED OFFERED TO help his mother sort and pack some of his father's things. Since he was their only child, his parents stayed near the base in a small house at Imperial Beach, California. The house was barely a thousand square feet, with just room enough for his mother's roses and the brightly-colored flowers she liked to grow year-round.

This year had taken a toll on her garden. She'd spent so much time at the Pirate's side in the hospital. The numerous close calls had gotten more frequent over the past two months before his passing, when she'd dropped everything and rushed to try to be there in time to send him off with a kiss.

Margaret Silver always said she had the greatest marriage in the whole world, although that same world knew it to be a complete fantasy.

"You know, Ned," she said as she began boxing books to take to the library sale, "in all the years we've been married, we never had a cross word. Not one."

Ned wasn't quite sure he'd heard her correctly. She had taken on some of Flo's air and penchant for coloring the truth to suit the moment. It was her way of spreading her brand of harmony over everything, just like those delicious peanut butter and jelly sandwiches she used to put in his Captain America lunch pail.

"You just never disagreed with him, Mom. You went along with anything he said."

"I was born to be married to Jake Silver. My job was to keep him operating within the lines he never wanted to look at," she said, fondly smiling at something out towards the distant ocean.

Ned had grown up riding the school bus that drove right past the obstacle course on Coronado, watching the men climb up those ropes like monkeys and wondering what it would feel like to ride in a little rubber raft while working with eight other souls to make sure it didn't capsize. He'd never considered doing anything else but join the Navy, like his dad.

But unlike his dad, Ned had become a SEAL. Old Jake had tried out twice and quit both times. When Ned got his Trident, his father didn't come to the ceremony and stayed drunk for a week.

Served the old bastard right.

He hadn't wanted to be there when his dad passed,

so when he came back from his last deployment, he was disappointed his stubborn dad was still alive. Checking his conscience, he didn't feel bad about one bit of it, either.

But his mother told him later Jake Silver had wanted to be sure he got home safe. He passed away the next day. That one did get to him. He had still been sore from the twenty hour transport plane ride and had planned to sleep for a week. Instead, he'd had to get out a suit he never wore, that still fit him after ten years. Duty and honor. That was it.

He had never brought friends over to the house for fear they'd find his dad in some undressed drunken state. Ned kept the secret, just like his mother did. Coach Silver was the most popular parent-coach on the Little League schedule. All the dads loved him, since short travel games were sources of some of the great parties the parents had, made better by the fact that his dad didn't have to pay for any of it. He was the coach. Number One.

The boys his own age idolized the former Navy man who had stories about slashing through jungles in Southeast Asia. Forbidden to read dirty magazines, the boys especially appreciated the tattoos of naked buxom ladies up and down his "Popeye" arms. His dad gave names for all of them and hinted he'd slept with each one. He was built like a bulldog and just staring down someone could stop a fight before it began.

Maybe it made him stronger. Ned didn't resent him. He just didn't want to be that kind of an imposition on anyone else. He loved working with his Team. And, as with many of the other guys he came to consider brothers on SEAL Team 3, being a SEAL was way more fulfilling than anything else he'd ever done. It gave him an outlet for his anger, being in such intense physical shape all the time, preparing for battle. Knowing he was responsible for each man on his right and his left, and that he would die to protect them gave him purpose. A strong, cohesive, unbreakable unit—he was part of something greater than he ever could be alone. They were a force for good. He could right some of the wrongs in the world and get paid and trained to do it too.

It was the perfect life. The bigger he got, the more muscle mass he put on, the faster and stronger he got, the less he resembled his father in anything they could be compared to. He was the exact opposite, determined to contribute more than his dad had ever done. It wasn't that he hated the man, he just left a big fucking hole. Old Jake left his mom damaged, but it was what she chose, and he'd agree with that, too. Yet that flaw was so great he couldn't even feel proud of his son.

So Ned's way of seeking his dad's approval was the opposite of his mother's. The more his dad didn't pay attention, the bigger and stronger he wanted to be.

Margaret Silver brushed the hair from her forehead and placed her hands at her hips. "Whew! That was a job. We did that in less than a quarter of the time I'd calculated."

"It helped that they were just old books neither of us wanted. Nothing to sort or ponder over, Mom."

"I don't even know why he had so many. I mean, this house is so tiny, and I never saw him read one of them. Did you?"

"I think he was going for the osmosis type of learning. Having them around him made him feel smarter. Maybe he learned without reading."

If ever a man could do that, his dad would be able to.

"I guess. It was always something I wanted to ask him, and I just forgot. Why he would want to hang on to books he never read will always be a mystery, then."

Ned stacked the last box near the front door. "Mom, should I load these up in the truck? I can drop them off at the library downtown tomorrow, if you like."

"Thank you, Ned." Then she noticed another small stack of books on the coffee table she'd set aside. "You know I thought perhaps you'd like these. The one on the top is a book of poetry about the sea. Maybe you should have it."

She held it out to him. He didn't want to take it but also couldn't turn it away.

"Okay, just this one. But all the rest of these are going to the library, no offense. I have less room in my condo than you do here."

"Fair enough." She smiled as he shoved the book into his back pocket. "I hope the library can take them. Lord knows I don't know what to do if they don't," she said as she opened the front door.

"They sell them, Mom. They make money for the library. So either way, it helps."

"That would be nice. See if you can get a slip of paper with the book count for our—my taxes this year."

"Will do," he said as he lifted the first box and headed toward his four-door pickup.

After they finished loading, he gently proposed they get started on his father's clothes. She hadn't touched a thing in their bedroom since the day he went to the hospital. His pills and water glass, still with water in it, sat beside the vanity sink in the bathroom. His slippers were tucked under the bed on his father's side. The bed on the other side was obviously slept in. His father's side had a fresh, ironed and unused pillowcase with eyelet trim, matching his mother's wrinkled one.

When Ned walked into the closet, he could smell the alcohol and the beer and cigars his dad liked to consume. Margaret sat on her side of the bed and watched him.

"Mom, where's your stuff?" Everything hanging up belonged to his father. His shirts were neatly pressed and starched, his pants hung on individual hangers, and even his bathrobe was hung with its cuffs tucked into the pockets as if it could walk on command.

"Over there," she said, pointing to the dresser.

Ned turned, his arm full of shirts, and examined the tall boy dresser with deep drawers. He had never realized all his mother's clothes were neatly folded inside, never hung up.

"Don't you have a coat? Any dresses?"

"They're in your bedroom closet, honey. I didn't like them smelling of cigars. It makes me sneeze."

Ned was struck by the fact that she still called it his bedroom. He'd visited them so infrequently over the past several years. Most of their get-togethers were done at a local restaurant, where his father's behavior was muted and under control.

He placed the stack of shirts on the bed behind her, while her fingers lovingly touched the buttons on the long-sleeved cuffs. "I'll drop these off at the Salvation Army too. I don't want to bag them, cause then they'll get wrinkled. But you kept these all ironed and starched, didn't you?"

"I love to iron. It soothes my mind."

That sounded just like Aunt Flo, and that scared

him. He retreated to the closet again, removing another stack of shirts and some slacks. He brought a large packing box and placed each pair of shoes carefully inside as she watched.

He knew she wouldn't have been able to do it on her own. Just before he was to carry out the box of shoes, he stooped to pick up his father's blue and green plaid slippers.

"Don't! Don't take those. I can wear those," his mother said.

"But Mom, they'll be too big for you. You'll trip. Why don't you let me get you a nice pair of women's slippers?"

"Ned, I want these," she said, her backbone showing. "I like the feel of them on my feet. And I'll be careful."

Ned tucked the slippers under the bed but on her side this time.

THEY SAT IN the tiny kitchen eating peanut butter and jelly sandwiches and canned soup. Ned had a beer, and his mother had a cup of tea. He'd never realized how small the house was. Growing up, it was just the place to sit, and do homework at night, or sleep. Ned's whole world was outside the doors and windows of the tiny home. His focus was never inside.

He'd also forgotten how quiet it was. The neighborhood had stayed modest, unlike other neighbor-hoods in the San Diego area. There were a lot of original couples, like his parents, who had bought when the subdivision was new and raised their families there. Kids could play out in the street until past dark or ride their bikes to the beach to watch the sunset. Anywhere important, he could go on a bike. Now, sitting in the sparse kitchen with his mother, he enjoyed the satisfying calm. That pit in the bottom of his stomach wasn't there. He didn't smell fear, because the generator of all those things was absent.

All that was left was the quiet.

As he drove away near sunset, he recalled the discussion he had with his mother. He stopped to watch the sun melt into the horizon, reached up, and held the mermaid pendant between his thumb and first two fingers.

He had thought the little place would be perfect for her now and offered to have some of the minor repairs done to make it easier. She could read, garden, or do whatever she wanted to now that she no longer needed to tend to his dad.

Her answer was odd. "But whatever will I do with myself?"

Ned had never wondered about that. She'd lost her job. Indefinitely furloughed and not needed. Even though old Jake was gone, she wasn't ready to stop being a wife and caretaker. Of course she would need some time to get back on her feet. She'd never considered another life.

"You have money, Mom. You could travel. Go on a cruise. Maybe you and Flo could take a train ride up north and see Canada."

"By ourselves? The two of us?"

"You could hire someone to go with you. Maybe one of the helpers at Flo's clinic would be available, like a companion nurse. Would that make it easier?"

"I don't think Flo would like going to strange places. She'd be confused all the time. I think it would be hard on her."

"You could room together. She could take the second bedroom here."

"Oh, no. I think we've got to face facts. Flo is going to need some full-time nursing. I'm going to look for a memory care center for her. I think in another few months she's going to stop remembering who I am. She has no friends, or at least none that she remembers. Your dad left me a little life insurance. If that's not enough I could sell the house."

"And then where would you live? Don't you want to stay here?"

She'd thought about it for several seconds before she answered.

"What if I went on an adventure, Ned?"

And like a turtle peeking out from under its shell for the first time, Margaret Silver wanted to see the real world. She wanted an adventure. He tried to hold back the hope that was springing from his chest, making him feel warm and glad to be among the living.

He walked across the sand to his truck after all remnants of the sun were gone. Driving the few miles to his condo complex, he knew the world had changed. The passing of his father had altered both his and his mother's trajectories.

Like falling from an airplane, he suddenly felt untethered, unrestricted, swimming through the blue sky toward an uncertain but somehow exciting future.

He grabbed the book of poetry but left everything else inside his truck and went inside his tiny box of a home, alone, but oddly happy.

CHAPTER 4

M ADISON RANG HER mother first thing in the morning and got no answer. She called the next-door neighbor, Mrs. Potter, whose cheerful voice annoyed her.

"Oh dear. I did see her yesterday morning. She was putting bird food out in the feeder. We have a terrible problem with the black crows and squirrels this year and they're scattering the seed everywhere, making a mess."

Madison cut her off or she'd get a description of the grime collecting on the insides of Mrs. Potter's washing machine.

"When was that?"

"I think it was about eleven. Maybe earlier. I didn't see her the rest of the day. She went for a walk afterwards, but came back an hour later."

"She was dressed, then, not looking ill?"

"Oh just like she always is. Wearing that bright-colored kimono over her black stretchies and that big red clip doing a piss-poor job of holding all that hair up. She had lipstick on, too, as I recall." Mrs. Potter began prattling on.

That relieved Madison a great deal. "I'll stop by to check on her later before I go to work. Thanks for the information."

"Should I stop by for a peek?"

"No, please don't."

Her mother had complained numerous times about her nosey neighbor, which is why Mrs. Potter was the first person Madison thought to call. If her mother was about, and dressed, then it ruled out so many awful things.

She took her coffee outside, checking the beach, which was beginning to warm up. The sunrise was long gone. Birds were slowly being replaced with beach-combers and scavengers looking for pieces of sea glass and colorful pieces of shells.

Barefoot and still wearing her favorite pair of stretchy pajamas, she walked in a straight line to the gentle surf. The water was calm, looking crystalline and transparent. September and October were her favorite months here on the gulf. The crowds were small, and the winds were mild between possible storm develop-ments. But the long, sunny, languid days were just the elixir she needed to stay sane and whole. The calm before the storms of life. She wondered if the storms she seemed to run into were just her way of fully embracing and enjoying the life-restoring calm of the ocean.

The beach heals everything, was still her favorite slogan, hanging in various forms in every room in her house, even the bedroom. Her mother had painted a huge one that still hung in her living room.

Madison sat, giving the cool surf a wide berth. She wasn't ready to get wet just yet. She watched an older couple walk hand-in-hand along the shore and mosey back to their address. It made her wonder about her mother and the mysterious someone special Noonan had mentioned last night. She knew studying her mother's face would tell her part of the story that would probably never be fully revealed.

Mother, what is this private world you live in and why do you leave me out?

She loved her as surely as she was sitting on the beach this morning. But she was a daughter to this magnificent woman, and that meant that her mother's embrace would only reach so far. And her mother's world of love would remain private no matter how much she tried to pry a little crack to sneak inside her womanly shell. She lived and taught Madison not with words, but by example. Unlike most women, her mother wore her flaws on the outside and saved her insides for the very best part of her.

Did you share yourself with this someone special?

Madison was convinced she did.

Noonan had said there might be salvage work coming up. That brought a smile to her face and a scurrying in her belly—that quest for the storm and excitement of an adventure. Diving around shipwrecks was always risky and never predictable. But the secrets they told of humanity long gone were fascinating. She loved delving into the mystery of loss and separation. It wasn't a morbid headspace. It celebrated the shadows of a life lived and now gone. Uncovering those secrets was like figuring out what had happened to her mother in the space of years that floated by before Madison was born.

Madison had had her little flings, mostly with older married men because it was safe. She could send them home to their wives transformed. She liked to think they were happier men and even their wives would benefit from the spark she brought to their lives.

Afterward, although she knew it wasn't common at all, her spirit was calm with the separation as she retreated to the land of her own making, alone and satisfied to be there. All the cliches aside, she was happy to be her own best friend, her own cheerleader, like all the books and gurus talked about. As long as she was free to swim in whatever blue ocean that lay before her. She knew she always would live by the sea, finding things discarded by the petulant being with an unpredictable energy. As long as she didn't fight, the ocean gave her everything she needed.

She twisted her bright blonde locks into a bun and walked through the cool ankle-depth waters, the waves washing away her footprints as if she'd never been there at all. She remembered the James Bond actor she met on the set of his new movie two years ago. Ruggedly handsome and tall, he was even better looking than how he appeared on the screen and Madison had seen every one of his movies. She was hired to be the body double for the villainess in the movie, the dark mermaid who would first make love to him and then try to kill him on an underwater dive. A evil, black siren.

Madison had to wear a cap glued with bits of dark black hair to hide her sundrenched locks that glistened like gold, even when wet. He was a good enough swimmer to do the takes with her. Back and forth they frolicked in one embrace after another, constrained by equipment and wetsuits, until the scene called for the two of them to emerge from the surf to strip and make love on the beach at sunset. It wasn't hard to feel what it would be like to wake up with him in her bed. And for several mornings they did just that. Nicer still that it was private—no black wig that might get dislodged, no one giving direction. Just the sound of their lovemaking and the background of the breathing ocean.

Her heartbeat raced as she remembered the incredible feeling of being the object of his desire, even though she knew it would only be for a week, maybe two. He made promises but she never did, knowing full well he'd never keep them. He promised to write, promised to stay in touch, promised to never forget her. That part she did believe. But as to the writing and keeping in touch, unless he was feeling her quickening libido, well, their magic would not stretch between Florida and Hollywood. Like a tender child growing up without the love of a parent, the magic would fade away into a beautiful memory like the clouds in the sky at sunset on Treasure Island.

She never looked him up on social media either. It didn't matter if she missed his encrypted message left so that only she would understand it. If she didn't look, she would never know. And she'd never be disappointed.

But a new film would be fun. Her heart could take one more big, epic romance before—what? She was speaking like a crazy woman. She was not thirty yet. Maybe for her birthday Poseidon himself would come to rescue her and take her below, shower her with jewels and gold, and keep her all for himself. Everyone would wonder. But she might like feeling she belonged to him, even if the world didn't know.

A true, private love would be something she could live for.

MADISON LIKED THE little artist community by the beach where her mother lived, mostly made up of old hippies and even beatniks from the Upper East Side in New York. Some of them were poets and had made and lost fortunes on their art, had it stolen or had managers abscond with all their loot. Living at the beach community of Treasure Island was a leveling out process where it didn't matter whether they were rich or poor. They had to have that inner spark, like her mother did. They had to have talent of some kind, some creative talent, or they were really good at making martinis or cooking a wild seafood pasta.

Madison had grown up with these people and had ridden on the shoulders of some who had graced the covers of Playbill, Vanity Fair, and Cosmo. They laughed reading the articles speculating where they'd disappeared to. Nobody came there looking for the rich and famous. Some were. Some weren't. And no one in the group cared.

Her mother had been in love with one or more of them, sometimes at the same time, which made for a confusing childhood. There were songs written about her. She'd taken in her share of broken, tarnished stars, polished them up, and sent them back out to shine again, hopefully living an inspired life.

Her dad would drift in every other year or so. He and her mom would do the tango, baiting each other to be the first one to fall in love again. Always one of them would, dragging the other one back into memories too sweet to ever forget. Then it would be all bedroom time and shouts and screams throughout the night followed by fights within three days and another separation. Then quiet.

"Ah, he's like the ocean. He comes in bearing gifts. Refreshed and ready to try the impossible again. He deposits his shells, takes a piece of me back with him, and disappears back out into the ocean to chase something else. It's his life, not the life I want. But he's hard to resist."

Madison had asked her if she loved him and why he didn't love her growing up.

"I'm his little girl, mama. Doesn't he care?"

"He's not capable. He wants to, but he can't get away from himself. But he made you and for that I'm eternally grateful."

Another time, she'd put it this way, "I love you, Madison. That's all you need to know. You don't want a man who doesn't know where he stands or isn't sure which wave he'll ride. You take the lighthouses in life. Sometimes they're boring as hell, but they'll always be there."

Except her mother never followed her own advice. Being hard to resist was always the most prominent feature of her love affairs, and often, the quality of her new love was held in highest regard. It was like the pull of the moon on the ocean. Only releasing to grab hold again. Dangerous and unpredictable. But yes, oh so irresistible.

Her mother would brush her long hair every night before bed. Just the two of them with the sight of the moon twinkling on the water beyond. The sound of her mother's brush and the warm feel of the boar bristles on her scalp were just as soothing as listening to the surf lapping on the sand all night long.

As she started puberty, she worried perhaps she had too much of a fixation for her mother, even going so far as to wonder if she perhaps loved her too much or was falling in love with women and not boys. But what Madison came back to time and time again was that one quality in her mother she found so special in a man.

Her mother was irresistible.

At her mother's cottage door, she knocked. Wind chimes started up as if recognizing the daughter coming home one more time. The alleyway leading down between modest and brightly colored shacks was covered in white rock and crushed shells. It was early for the beach, and only a stray dog wandered along the path.

Her mom had painted her house a deep rose color, trimmed in vanilla. A large vine with bright purple-pink flowers was holding up the overhang above the front door. Madison noticed that someone had tried to paint in between the crisscrossing vines that wrap themselves around the wood bracing like Sleeping Beauty's castle, but had given up. She wondered how long that had been there, but it was the first time she'd noticed it.

Madison knocked again.

She heard music, which grew louder as her mother graced the doorway with a bright, warm smile. "What a nice surprise!"

That's what she always said. But she knew her mother meant it every time. It would take her several minutes before she could untangle herself from her mother's arms. Her big grey hair was tied up with a bandana ending in a floppy bow at the upper right side of her forehead.

"I'm painting again, Madison. Come! Let me show you."

The one thing Madison had loved about this house was the great room off the kitchen that faced the ocean. They'd had large dinners where they'd moved all the furniture out and brought in folding chairs and served over thirty on occasion. But everything about the back of the house was focused on the ocean, facing west.

In past years, Madison's old room had also been the craft room. Often, she'd wake up and work on sewing or painting projects, sometimes working until dawn. After Madison moved out, her mother returned it to the library it had been before she was born. With two high-backed chairs facing each other, the room was so filled with books that it totally insulated the sounds of anything else, even the traffic outside and calls from the ocean. Many nights she'd stop by late for a visit and find her mom curled up in one of those chairs asleep with a book in her lap and a fuzzy afghan around her shoulders.

But now the living room was packed with brightly colored canvases depicting beach scenes peppered with colorful shacks and crushed shell trails. She was working on several at once, just like the history of her love life.

"You're going big, Mom. How long have you been doing these?"

"I just started yesterday morning. I stayed up all night long painting. Remember when we used to have those marathons, honey? I've got my mojo back!"

Madison didn't cheer because she wasn't sure where this was all going.

"What brought all this on?"

"I smell Fall in the air. I was feeling just a bit down,

frumpy. Very low energy. It was like all the fun had been taken out of life. I got fed up and decided to do something I hadn't done. So, I walked the neighborhood until I found inspiration. I went to the art store and bought all the large canvases they carried. Bought some new brushes and acrylic paints I'd never tried before. I was seeing flowers, pretty houses all in a row. This place I love." She smirked at her daughter. "You don't believe me, do you?"

"No, it sounds exactly like you, Mom."

"This house holds the soul of my life. I've forgotten to celebrate it lately. That's what I'm doing now."

Madison was heartened with the news. Her mother wasn't old, barely sixty, and was very attractive still, though her attractiveness was—yes, there it was again—in her irresistibility! She did have some of the sparkle back. As she thought about it, Madison had noticed some kind of glum smoke bomb hanging over her head lately.

"I'm glad. I worried. You didn't answer your phone this morning."

"I turned it off so I didn't ruin the inspiration."

"Yes, well, your usual appearance last night at the Dog was missing. You were missed. Noonan missed you too."

"Noonan? Gosh, I haven't talked to him in months. What's he up to?"

"He says he might have work for me. A special dive. I wish it was a film."

"Oh that was a once in a lifetime event, Maddie. Those are like glass ornaments on your Christmas Tree of life." She picked up a brush and pointed to her. "Something to be celebrated!"

Then Madison remembered Noonan's words.

"He had a message for you."

"Who? Noonan? I hope he's not considering trying to court again. This shop is closed while I explore my new full throttle mojo experience!"

Madison stepped closer to her mother and whispered, "He says someone special has passed. He said you'd know what that meant."

CHAPTER 5

NED GATHERED WITH several other members of their team at the Rusty Scupper, their local Team hangout. Kyle, his LPO, was present, along with Cooper and T.J., but all the other guys were single or divorced, so it was mostly an unofficial pre-bachelor party. One of the newbies had gotten engaged. The divorced SEALs gave him advice, since this was his first rodeo.

One of the first things any newbie did when they came to the Scupper was check out the Wall of the Fallen, originally over the bar but now nearly covering the back wall—a private "meeting" room with pictures of campaigns and team flags and mementos. Ned always swung through there if it had been awhile, just to check out if something new had been added. Sometimes the pictures were hard to find, like the time he discovered the photograph of a warlord they'd captured that the military had tried and executed. His disheveled face, with his hands tied in front of him in a dirty, wrinkled shirt and his hair all askew looked completely different than the military man they'd seen on TV with his chest covered in medals he earned while slaughtering, not protecting his people.

The room was a shrine to who they were and what they stood for. To the average person, it might seem like some kind of sick reverence, but for every one of these bad guys they'd captured or killed—which wasn't the goal like it had been years ago—thousands of American and Allied soldiers would be safer, as well as scores more of their own citizens. It was for the little people they fought. Not for the big wigs. Not even the big wigs in the military. After all, they were a force for good. There were bad guys lurking in the halls everywhere.

He took a seat at the table, which was already knee-deep in advice to the new groom-to-be.

"Make sure she shows up at the bonfires, man. She needs to make friends amongst the wives, not outside, or you'll have trouble," someone said.

Kurt, the newbie medic-in-training, looked no more than eighteen years old. His eyes were big, and his ears stuck out as if shaving had made them more prominent. Ned could tell he was nervous as hell about the wedding but even more apprehensive of the bachelor party these guys were going to throw.

It was legend, but rarely occurred, that sometimes grooms were sent away the night before the wedding, drunk, with a one-way ticket to someplace in Alaska or Greenland. But just the fact that it had occurred once or twice, causing brides and her parents to have a reception without the groom, later to be followed up with a civil ceremony, made many of the young, newly-engaged SEALs worry. And the stories were embellished and expanded to such a degree that no one could remember exactly who these fiascos had befallen. They became things of urban legend, a weapon the older guys used to mess with the heads of the tadpoles.

Coop decided to intervene. "Nah, kid, don't listen to those guys. As a matter of fact, don't listen to anybody who's divorced or not happily married after a divorce. You'll ruin your career and your love life if you spend too much time hanging with them." He pointed to the other end of the table with his mineral water and lime.

That caused a ruckus as the hardcore group objected.

Ned sat still, not having much of an opinion, which Kyle noticed.

"I'm sorry about your dad, Ned. Christy called you?"

"Yes, she did. Thanks, Kyle."

"I was real sorry. I try to get to all my guys things

like that, but the briefing in D.C. took longer. I'd have rather been at your side."

"No problem. I totally understand. I was there mostly for my mom anyway. My dad and I weren't that close."

Kyle nodded, tracing the bubbles scurrying up the side of his beer glass. "A common reflection, Ned."

The two of them listened to more of the banter before Kyle added, "You did good over there this time, Ned. You're turning into a lifer."

Ned shrugged. "Never thought I'd spend so much time in Africa. When I signed on, it was all Middle East stuff. Now, things have changed."

"The world is changing. We're changing our focus as a country too. Personally, I think we'll see more things in the Caribbean and South America coming up. I think the training missions are a complete waste of time, teaching the bad guys how to kill us best."

"I don't miss those. Although, sometimes they were fun. I guess some people were just not meant to carry telephone poles and wade around in little boats." He was referencing a group of young recruits from Greece who had gotten shipped into a BUD/S class and refused to do any of the hard labor, especially the twelve-man teams carrying telephone poles down the beach. They didn't earn a Trident, just a certificate, but none of the men thought they even deserved that.

"Wish I had some videos to show the head shed," Kyle mumbled. Then he asked, "You plan on taking any time to do something special?"

"Nothing planned as yet. I'm helping my mom get her place cleaned up. You know, get all my dad's stuff out. It's hard for her."

"I'll bet. How long were they married?"

"I think they were pregnant when they did, so I guess thirty-one or thirty-two years. At least thirty."

"Well, your mom will get on her feet. You'll see. If they were happily married, she'll get married again. Just you wait."

Ned chuckled.

"What's so funny?"

"It's a matter of perspective. Honestly, Kyle, my dad was an asshole. My mom loved him anyway. Through her perspective, they had the greatest love story in the world."

"Yeah. I sure hope Christy doesn't have to fantasize like that with me." Kyle took another drink. "How about you, Ned? I never see you bring anyone to our gatherings."

He shrugged again. He was doing a lot of that lately. "I'm thinking I'll be more like Tierney. Heck, he was older than me when he got married. Worked out okay for him. I think I might have to retire before I settle down. It would be complicated trying to have a family and do what we do. But that's just me."

Kyle nodded again and then slapped him on the back. "Well, then you stay single, hear? We need men like you. And while you're at it, keep an eye on Kurt here and make sure he doesn't wind up on a detour flight with a couple of hookers. He doesn't deserve that."

Ned chuckled again. "No one deserves that."

ALTHOUGH HE'D PROMISED otherwise, right after Kyle and Cooper left, he abandoned the bachelor group and headed for his condo. He was tired. But he knew it wasn't from any physical workout or regimen. It was from a whole lot of emotional energy he'd expended taking care of his mom. She was going to need some assistance before he would stop worrying about her.

Tomorrow, she was going to visit a new memory center that had been built just north of San Diego where patients participated in advanced clinical trials, the stay partially being underwritten by a couple of large drug companies looking for cures for dementia and Alzheimer's. He was proud she was taking such a measured approach, and although she'd invited him to come along, he knew he would be more needed when it was time to actually take Aunt Flo there. He promised her that. This was something she had to do on her own, he said, and she agreed.

All the boxes had been dropped off today at the thrift store and library. He washed his truck, went for a short workout before heading to the Scupper, and then decided to retire early.

His condo was very sparsely furnished. He just couldn't decide what to buy and the down payment on the place had eaten up all his enlistment bonus, which left him with just a thin margin of savings. Like his old place living at home, his focus was never inside his small space, but outside. The reason he'd bought the condo was because it had a view of the water. A tiny sliver, but a view anyhow. He'd paid a twenty thousand dollar premium for that view. And he loved the bright orange and pink sunsets.

He grabbed the book he'd brought from his mom's house, slunk back into his couch, and propped his feet up on the coffee table.

The small paperback was dog-eared. It looked like some do-it-yourself publication without a lot of fancy embellishments or anything on the back cover but another picture of a long, white sand beach.

'Gifts From The Sea'

He read farther, *'A compilation of short stories and poetry from the Gulf Coast.'*

Ned knew his dad had a friend who lived there still. He was the buddy who had partnered with him that day when his dad found the pendant. Ned had been to several trainings on the east coast of Florida, probably near the old Spanish Galleon wreck they'd explored. He remembered seeing a map of the coastline littered with wrecks, some of them with undiscovered treasure. His dad told him he loved it there. Ned wondered why the family hadn't moved to Florida, since it would have been so much less expensive.

But for some reason, Pirate Jake stayed away and let himself go.

Inside the back cover flap was a picture of a group of young people standing in a cluster with parrot drinks in their hands, toasting the camera. On the photo credit, Ned saw his father's name.

'Photo courtesy of Pirate Jake Silver.'

Suddenly, Ned was interested. He flipped through the pages, letting his fingers smooth over the paper, scanning the short stories and poems written by different people with names he didn't recognize. He came to a page that had been folded over.

'Amberly'

It was written by a man named Darrell and was a glowing, gushing description of a woman named Amberly who had captured his heart. He described her swimming through the water and lying in the sand. Without being overtly sexual, it was a passionate piece and hinted of deep intimate knowledge. He likened her to a beautiful mermaid he could never capture.

Ned knew his dad liked this piece. He wondered if this was his dad's mermaid as well, the secret love he'd whispered about so long ago, embodied and captured in the silver pendant that was the only thing his dad had given him unselfishly.

He glanced at other poems and saw one written by Amberly Drake.

I am following so close I fear you'll see me,
And the secret love I hold will be revealed,
Before I can even bring the words to my lips.
Is it true that you can fall in love,
The first time you look into someone else's eyes,
And feel their soul meld with yours?
As one who is used to seeing the door close behind
    those I've loved,
This time it will hurt.
Forever.

CHAPTER 6

MADISON HADN'T WANTED to leave her mother, but she was due to be at work, and they'd had several no-shows lately with the wait staff.

Her mother's face had gone from a look of pure delight to that split-second expression of horror, followed by her quick adjustment as she donned her mask and covered up all feeling, which wasn't her usual style. Madison knew it was self-preservation. No amount of inquiry would bring out what her mother wouldn't tell her. It was hard to do, but she had to be good with it. Her mother promised she might stop by later on and asked if she could tell Noonan to look for her.

It was past the lunch crowd, a lull before the early diners, usually older patrons, came for the seafood specials. Washington Jones was meting out his private brand of fear on the younger Latino kitchen help, working his way through the usual turnover statistics.

With the clanging of pots and pans and shouts, it was murder and mayhem in that hot little kitchen—barely big enough for Jones' girth, let alone other man-boys trying to avoid crashing into him with their platters of food prep.

The sounds were oddly calming. Normal life.

She stocked the bar, and wiped down the countertop and all the stools again, even though it had been done by the previous crew. She cleaned all the tables and cleared someone's salad lunch that had been forgotten. All of this felt like gardening, painting, or walking along the beach, these simple routines that gave her time to think. Funny how cleaning up someone else's mess was soothing to her, but it was.

There was a new musician playing tonight, and he came in early to make sure everything was set up properly so he could start at five. He'd come highly recommended by a friend when they watched him perform at another crabby joint along the peninsula.

He was tall and extremely handsome, slightly older with grey hair at his temples. His quiet demeanor and wonderful manly scent didn't overpower her. It did make her long for the arms of someone who could cherish her, even if it was for one night.

His sly smile and dimpled chin were disarming, not that she was putting up any resistance.

Garrison Cramer was a born horse trainer, if there

ever was one. Her heart raced, and she tried not to let their eye contact linger or he'd get the message she wasn't ready to deliver.

"You get a big crowd on Fridays?" he asked as he set his guitar against the stand.

Madison had been re-wiping the tables out on the patio near his "stage" right in front of the dartboard and several other children's games.

"Yes, it's one of our busiest. But this time of year, the snowbirds haven't returned, so it's mostly locals getting their fill of the nice beach vibe after the craziness of the summer, and before the craziness of the holidays."

"That mean you're local?"

She held out her hands, one clutching her wet rag, the other with her spray bottle of cleaner, "That's me. Born and raised." She wanted to ask where he was from but pegged him for some place in the South. He didn't have a Florida accent, and he definitely wasn't Texas.

"Good to know."

Okay, dammit. She had to ask. "You're from Tennessee, North Carolina or—"

"All over. I've lived in Nashville, Memphis, Mobile, Atlanta—you name it. I've played there."

She decided to give him slight encouragement and just play it out. "One of the original rolling stones, then, is that right?"

"Yes, ma'am," he said softly.

His words hit her chest like the gentle gulf wind. Then he raised the stakes.

"At your service."

He probably noticed she'd grabbed a plastic menu and fanned herself. She couldn't look him in the eyes any longer because it was going too fast. But that had never been a problem before. This quiet man was taking full control.

"More of that where it came from, darlin'."

Her little smile was pathetic. "I'll bet. Well, you make a helluva introduction. Don't you give a lady time to adjust herself?"

He slowly perused up and down her body and whispered, "No adjustment needed. But I would like your phone number, if you don't mind."

That was a little over the top, and she needed the breather. "How about we settle for a crab salad, as promised and on the house, and then we can take care of that business later?"

"Suits me fine. Am I allowed a beer? Just one?"

"Monty has a policy he allows one an hour, but if you fall off that stool, you're done."

"No problem. I'll be in full control."

I'll bet.

She turned to go when he called after her. "By the way, I'm Garrison Cramer. And you are?"

"I'm Madison." She turned quickly before her cheeks flamed further and heard his soft whisper behind her back.

"Of course you are."

MADISON'S EARS BUZZED every time she looked at the handsome singer perched on the stool on the patio, who had the ear of everyone in the room, including just about all the ladies, both young and old. If there ever was a troubadour, who could wiggle women out from behind their wedding vows, he was the right kind of sweet-sounding, buttery-tongued devil well practiced at it. It was such a welcome change.

She counted her lucky stars. She was about to take on a new adventure and perhaps a new adventure with her heart as well. Things were beginning to feel exciting. Instead of regretting her threshold of thirty—when the doorway between youth and the beginnings of aging begins to sound alarms—she was headed right into a storm, willing to tether herself to the mast of a handsome, perhaps dangerous, stranger.

Their eye contact was smoldering but infrequent. He was good at giving the same look to several other ladies in the audience, too, and that became less attractive as the second and third hour passed. It didn't preclude some experimentation. However, she wasn't going to chase.

Noonan sauntered in, wearing a fresh pair of jeans and a long-sleeved, even ironed shirt with snap buttons on the cuff and cowboy boots. It was not the beach vibe she was used to seeing him in and it made Madison convinced her mother must have called him. He was definitely dressed up.

Even his patch was clean.

"Hey there, dearie. Your mom been by yet?"

"So she called you?"

"She left a message. I was indisposed." He wiggled his eyebrows. "Can I have a beer? My usual."

"Sure, Noonan. Shall I put it on your regular tab too?"

"Nah, I brought money tonight. I'm going to try to talk your mother into having dinner with me."

Madison checked her cell. "At eleven o'clock? She doesn't eat that late."

"Says who?" Madison heard her mother's voice from behind. "When I was your age I ate all the time, it seems."

She looked gorgeous. Reds and oranges were her best colors. Her grey hair, streaked with light and dark patches, was confined to a neat, French roll at the back of her head. She wore turquoise jewelry she'd bought once in Arizona, the squash blossom pieces looking opulent and over the top as they contrasted against the rose reds and oranges of her oversized silk scarf, covering a black top over black jeans. Neither one of them looked like beach people. They looked like tourists.

Or people on their first date.

Her mother flashed the one-eyed pirate a wide smile Madison hadn't seen since this morning. Whatever had happened with the news about the "special person," she was over it and moving on with gusto.

"Hello, Noonan."

"Amberly. Looking mighty fine." He watched to see if she liked his comment before he followed it up with a sexy smile.

"As do you," she said as she looked away quickly. "Maddie dear, can I have a beer?"

Madison gave her the same Red Flamingo beer Noonan preferred. The two aging, former lovers clinked glasses and moved to a table out of earshot of Madison. It didn't take more than thirty seconds before her mother reached out across the table and gripped Noonan's hand. Their bodies leaned across too for a private chat. She had never seen Noonan so attentive or sober.

As the evening drew to a close, her mother and Noonan were still talking. Neither one of them had eaten much of their dinners and finally directed them to be removed. The rowdy crowd had started to arrive. The music was coming to a close, soon to be replaced with some canned country greatest hits that the crowd could dance to under the warm Florida night.

And, probably because she'd been distracted with the steady stream of drinks she was pouring for the thirsty crowd and straining to hear whatever was being discussed between her mother and the Pirate, Garrison Cramer was chatting up two very young lovelies. Their eye contact had ceased, and it was clear her vision for a night of awesome sex was completely out the window.

He did give her another one of those sexy smiles as he rounded the bar, his arm over both their shoulders on his way out. "You workin' tomorrow?"

"Maybe," she said, making a fake attempt at stubbornness.

"Then maybe I'll see you. Until then, be good."

She watched the three of them exit the bar area with envy. After their car left the parking lot, she noticed she'd been grinding her teeth.

Noonan appeared at the bar with his arm around her mother's waist. "Hey, kid. I just wanted you to know that I paid my bill this time." He winked. His nose had turned bright red, and she hoped, wherever they were going, although she had a pretty good idea they might be headed to her mom's cottage at the beach, that her mother was driving.

"You even left a tip. Iris told me," she answered.

"And he didn't use my credit card, either," added

her mother.

"Maddie, I got the official word about the dive. We start Wednesday, so get two, maybe three days off if you can. I'm putting together a crew now." He smiled down on her mother's face and then added, "I think you'll like who I'm going to invite to come along."

"James Bond?"

"Nope. It's a secret."

"Great. I'll let Monty know tonight. Where is it?"

"It's a barge. Went down about two hundred years ago, delivering molasses and staples en route to Tampa Bay from Cuba."

"A barge? No passengers?"

Noonan winked. "We're not looking for passengers. We're looking for the cook's dog."

"After two hundred years?"

He smiled. "Well, not exactly the dog. The dog's collar. That's the prize."

CHAPTER 7

NED'S MOTHER CALLED him the next morning letting him know that the memory care facility had an immediate opening for Aunt Flo and wondered if he could help move her.

"Normally, the wait time is over six months. But they just had someone leave, and it's ours if I can get her over there by five."

"Will she cooperate?" he asked.

"It depends on how it's done. That's why I want you there. She still remembers you rather vividly. For me, sometimes, there can be a tug of war. She knows I control most of her finances and her life. When she's conscious to understand that, the bits and pieces that come through are sometimes scrambled."

"Okay, I'll be there as soon as I can."

"I have the board and care home collecting her things, boxing them up discreetly."

"I'm on my way."

When he arrived, all Hell had broken loose. When Flo came back from lunch and scoped the boxes and all the packing, she left the facility, heading out a rear exit door that had remained unlocked. The staffers had searched everywhere, hoping to find her nearby.

Ned looked for some trace of where she'd gone, assuming she'd left by the exit.

"Isn't this close to your house, Mom?" he asked.

"It is. But it's still about twenty blocks away. That's a half mile."

"I'm wondering if she's trying to make it back to your place."

"I'm not thinking she could ever figure that out. Not sure I could either," his mom said.

"What exactly happened?"

"It was the packing, all the boxes and stuff," one of the staffers said.

"That must've totally freaked her out. How could you have let that happen?" he asked.

"You know how it goes. They were supposed to hold her in the dining hall then take her to her mailbox and the library for a short film. Instead, she got loose, walked in here, grabbed her coat and gloves, and was out the door before we could catch her."

"That's why she needs a facility more for her memory than anything else," said his mother, worry laced in her voice. "She's very mobile and strong. And she looks very normal. If somebody didn't know better, they might even let her drive, you know?"

Ned's alarm bells went off like a fire station. "Yeah, that would be a danger to her and everyone else."

"The problem for me, of course, is that I've always sort of been the one to look over her, and I've had to come to the conclusion that there's a limit to what I can do. I have to face the fact that she needs expert help, something way beyond what I'm trained for."

"You've got no argument from me." Ned turned to the two male attendants. "You got any ideas?"

"If she went out the back, I'm thinking she'd stay off the road. But all the yards are fenced on this side."

"What about beyond the yards?"

"Nothing?"

"As in what?"

"No houses. Just a thick brush. Weeds. Deer and raccoons, that kind of stuff."

Ned and the male nurses wandered up and down the back of the large property. Then he remembered that there had been a small creek running by his mother's house and wondered if it also ran behind the board and care. He directed the two staffers to follow behind.

They scaled a chain-link fence, walked through dense brush, and came upon a homeless encampment set up under the trees, tucked away so that it was invisible to any neighbor or street nearby. The encampment had tents, bicycles, and even a patio umbrella. He heard a radio playing in the background.

In the middle of a semi-circle of several transient males was Aunt Flo. She was decked out to the nines, wearing her Sunday best, including white gloves. It was a scene he never thought he'd see. He walked up behind Flo, put his finger to his lips so that the other men seated at the circle wouldn't reveal his approach.

"Hey, Aunt Flo, it's great to see you!"

Just when she turned, he put his hand gently on her shoulder and gave her a big grin.

"Oh, Ned!" she said as she rose. "We were looking for you everywhere! Your mother was worried sick!" She extended her hand toward the group of males in an attempt to begin introductions. "My memory sometimes fails me fellows, so could you tell me your names again, please?"

The group stared at each other and, one by one, began to rise slowly. One of them was on crutches, and another had an artificial leg from the mid-calf down.

"Kennie."

"I'm Regis."

"I'm Army Daniels. From San Diego."

"My name is Boris, and I am from Russia. Nice to meet you." He gave a quick bow, then added, "We weren't quite sure what to do, but we figured someone would come along looking for her. We were prepared to take her to the police."

Ned reassured them. "No problem, gents. You guys did the right thing. I'm glad you didn't get her scared." He put his hand on Flo's shoulder again "Sometimes she gets scared, doesn't remember where she is. Isn't that right, Aunt Flo?"

Flo rolled her eyes, swatted the air in front of her face and addressed her group of comrades still standing in the circle. "Isn't it just like a man? You look all over for them, and when they finally pop up, they act like *you're* the one who was lost!"

Several of the men chuckled. One spat a black gob of phlegm. Boris didn't say anything.

The peg-leg homeless man said, "You go with your nephew now, Flo. I'll let the two of you work things out, okay?"

His reaction seemed to please her. "This has been a lovely visit, gentlemen. Next time I will bring you all some of my very best lemonade and chocolate chip cookies. Will you guys be here tomorrow?"

They looked between themselves, and all five of them nodded their heads.

NED RACED WITH the two women north to Flo's new home, hoping to reach it by five o'clock. They had brought as much as he could carry in the back of the truck, covered by a tarp. The rest of her things, he would pick up later and have delivered.

Flo went without incident. She loved road trips and excitedly talked about her new friends and what a nice garden they tended. Ned was never surer that his mother was doing the right thing, even that perhaps it was long overdue.

About five miles outside San Diego, his aunt fell asleep against the window, on the driver's side behind Ned. He thought about bringing up the poetry book he'd studied last night and decided against it. The air was already thick with things unsaid.

His mother broke her silence first.

"Ned, you're going to get a call from a friend of your father's. His name is Noonan LaFontaine, the former Navy diver your dad served with and spent some time with in the Florida Keys before you were born."

"The guy who was with him when he found this," he said as he held out the pendant.

"The very same. He wasn't able to attend the funeral, but he wanted to express his condolences, and he's invited you to come out and spend a week or two with him in Florida."

"Not sure I can get the leave, Mom."

"Well, you think about it. I gave him your cell." Before he could protest, she'd already given him the palm of her hand. "I know. But in a way, he's family. Not by blood, but he and your dad had a bond."

Ned wasn't sure he wanted to spend any time around someone who was close to his father. But he was more than curious if this fellow was one of the little groups in the picture from that poetry book. He also considered the possibility that his dad was someone different in Florida than he was in San Diego.

"Don't do that anymore, Mom. You know you're not to give out my phone, my picture, or anything about me."

"Yes, yes, I know. This is different." She continued. "I think you should go, that's all. Flo will hopefully be settled. You've helped me. You've just gotten back from overseas. Take a little time, a little beach time. Your dad always drew a great deal of strength from the beach."

"Are you talkin' about *my* dad? The pirate bastard?"

"He wasn't always that way. We were so happy when you came along. Everything was perfect. We laughed at your antics. He was a different man then." She watched the countryside stream by, the gentle rolling hills, still brown and unrecovered from the hot summer. Between expanses of dead were bright green rows of tended gardens. It was a huge flower-growing region with peaceful, uncluttered farmland, looking the way it probably did a hundred years ago.

"This isn't going to be one of those surprises like, 'Hey, he's your dad' or anything is it?"

His mother in profile smiled, shaking her head. Then she turned to face him. "I've only ever slept with one man, and that man was your father."

"The Pirate bastard, not this Noonan guy, right?"

"Right."

"Okay, I'll talk to him. Just trying to get my bearings here."

She chuckled. "He used to say that all the time. I used to laugh every time he'd say it, because for all his planning and calculating, when he was sailing in those days, he always managed to get lost. It was sort of our joke. He planned so hard only to get lost, whereas everyone else on the planet just got lost."

He could feel the lid on her personality curling at the edges as if she was gradually releasing something she'd kept bottled up. In another place, in another lifetime, she might have been a completely different person.

LATER THAT NIGHT, Ned got the call he'd been expecting.

"I'm a friend of your father's," said the crusty voice of someone who could have been his father's twin.

"I've heard some of the stories, Mr. LaFontaine. I'm

just—"

"Oh, this is far more than about your dad, Son. I've been contracted to do a special dive for a private individual to look for an artifact that was sunk some two hundred years ago off the *gulf* side of Florida. I'm hiring a team, and as a former SEAL, I know you've got some great experience. That's what I need."

"I'm still active, Mr. LaFontaine, but I've never done anything like that. The equipment is all different."

"No, it's not. Mine just has more stickers and stuff. It's more beat-up because I don't have a rich Uncle Sam. And of course, you wouldn't be bringing yours. You'd use mine, Son."

"When are you going out?"

"We start Wednesday."

"You have full permission?"

"Yup. Florida's signed off. We're below the monetary limit anyway. We're looking to get something more sentimental than valuable."

"How deep?"

"It's shallow. Way less than a hundred feet. Probably sixty to eighty. Lots of people have gone after things there, but the storms this year really pushed things around, scrambled the wrecks, so it could be deeper, but not by much that close to the coastline. It will be warm, so we'll wear our shorties. I'm not bringing anyone on who doesn't have a lot of experience. And, in case you're wondering, I don't dive any longer. I'm the captain."

"Have you calculated the weather for next week?"

"Are you kidding? It's gorgeous this time of year. Not a hurricane in sight, not yet. We'd have lots of warning. And this isn't the Caribbean, you know. Not that unexpected stuff. You've been there, of course."

"I have."

"Well, this will be like diving in a nice, warm swimming pool. Crystal clear water and not mucked up with overpopulation. Just all the things you like about the ocean. We're keeping to all the rules. This isn't a pirate mission, despite what you may have heard about me."

"Yeah, I heard so many stories I stopped believing in them long ago."

"That's a shame. Your dad was a helluva guy and an even better storyteller."

"Said no one ever in California."

Noonan chuckled, which led him into a coughing fit. "Sinuses," he said by way of explanation. It sounded like full-on bronchitis to Ned.

"So you and Mom kept in touch, then?"

"No, not really. I never met her. I kept in touch with your dad, but the last time I talked to him was from the hospital. He'd borrowed someone's cell. He told me all kind of nice things about you. But come out here, and I'll tell you all about it, if you're interested."

Ned had to admit he was. Although he had no burning desire to know more about his dad's past, he was interested in the area. He too had loved the Florida weather, the coast, and the vibe of the little beach towns he'd visited on the Atlantic side, where they'd done most of their training. He decided to test for Noonan's sense of humor.

"So you sure you're not my dad? If secrets are being revealed, I just wanted a little forewarning."

Noonan nearly coughed himself to death. "Shit no. Your dad would have killed me if I'd ever laid a hand on that woman." After Ned didn't respond, Noonan added, "But knowing your dad as I do, I don't blame you for asking. I'll be able to tell the first time I see you if your mama messed around with anybody else. You'd be old Jake's boy. Like it or not, you'd look just like him. I know you would."

Ned was sold but didn't want to let the old captain know. "I'll think about it."

"Nope. If you say no, then I've got someone else to call. That's the way we roll here. I'm not here to drag you to the beautiful Florida coast. You gotta feel like coming, like you're being led on a strange new adventure. Quit the stuff in your head, and just come on over. We'll sort out the rest of the world another day, hear me?"

"Yessir, I do."

"So you'll fly into Tampa, and I'll pick you up when you text me your flight."

"Where will I stay?"

"Well, that's up to you, but you're welcome to reside on the boat, or you can room in town, Treasure Island. There are a bunch of little vacation rentals available. I can see if I can fix you up. Can you spend like $50 a day on a place?"

"That's doable."

"Then no problem."

"Alright then. I'll text you when I get it arranged. When do you want me?"

"As soon as you can get here. Doesn't matter to me, as long as you're flexible with the accommodations."

"Sounds good. Gotta check in with the Team and then I'll let you know when."

"Glad to have you aboard. Oh, and one last thing, you'll get paid three hundred dollars a day, but not until we find what we're looking for. That's the deal. But I'll provide all the gear and chow when we're out. Okay?"

Ned called Kyle next and got the okay to leave for ten days. He checked online for flights out of San Diego and found a direct one to Tampa. He got out his black duffel bag, leaving his heavy equipment tucked inside the safe bolted to the floor of his condo. He began packing trunks and a couple of nicer shirts just in case some nice seafood dinners were in the offing.

He could finish tomorrow. But just in case he forgot, he placed the little book of poetry on top of the clothes already in the bag.

It was his ticket on his new ride, the roadmap to help get him lost, just like his father had done so many years ago.

CHAPTER 8

MADISON'S MOM ASKED her to join her for lunch before she went to work. She found her mother out on the beach, seated in the sand, throwing rocks and pieces of shells into the surf. The day had turned out slightly overcast, so it wasn't overly hot.

Madison sat right next to her. "I'm guessing you had a fairly nice evening last night. When you guys are getting along, you make the finest looking couple." She threw her arm around her mother's shoulder and drew their bodies close then released her.

"Noonan's an acquired taste. He can be charming, or he can be just downright irritating. I like him both ways, but only when he's irresistible."

There was that word again!

"Well, I'm happy for you."

Her mother continued tossing rocks and shells into the surf. Madison could tell she was trying to figure something out, and once she did, there was going to be a proclamation.

"So what did you want to talk about?"

"Can't I have lunch with my daughter?"

"Yes, but twice in two days?"

"Just humor me. These are strange times."

Madison decided she'd take the more direct approach. "Can I ask you who the '*someone special*' was? The one you and Noonan were talking about?"

"He was special." She squinted at the horizon. The combination of escaping sun from behind a silver cloud and the gentle breeze off the ocean made her eyes water. Madison didn't think for a minute she was crying.

"He was one of those men you meet probably once-in-a-lifetime. I think I knew these last few days that he was leaving this world. There was just heaviness in the air. I was feeling tired, like something inside me was dying too. I actually think it's like that with some special people, don't you?"

Madison knew that the only person she could ever feel this way about would be when the time came for her mother to pass on. But she didn't want to utter it, for fear of making it so. She was well aware that the universe was a fragile place.

"You've got me there, Mom. I've never met anyone like that in my life. So I'm going to have to defer to your experience."

"I'm going to be spending a lot of time here looking at the ocean. It's all I can do."

"Are you okay? I mean, should you be alone?"

"I'm not alone. I've got the Crabby Crew—my friends. Heck, even if I did want to be alone, they'd never let me. There's always time for celebration, song, and good wine with that crew. You've met them."

"Yes, I know them very well. You're blessed, Mom." Madison hesitated to say it. "And you've got Noonan too. He doesn't mind hanging around, I'm sure."

"Noonan!" She threw a larger smoothed rock into the surf after barking his name. "Last night was about sharing grief, healing. Having someone close who is going through the same thing, someone familiar around you to take away the vacantness. He did his job well, God love him."

Madison thought that was a beautiful way to describe her friendship with the old sea captain. "So not just for the sex," she whispered.

"Not hardly. We'd have needed more alcohol for that. Maybe some dancing. No, this was communion. Healing each other because we could."

Madison could see the two of them were on the same wavelength.

"That's enough!" her mother finished. She stood, leaned over, and gave Madison her hand. "Come on.

Let's go inside and have a bite."

She'd set a table with fresh Gloriosa Daisies in the middle, the bright yellow sunshine cheering the whole place up. She'd made a salad, chilled, and added fresh crabmeat to the top just before serving. She knew it was Madison's favorite.

"Do you want some white wine?"

"I'm good." Madison waited for her mother to sit down and then continued her questions. "So when Noonan said he was gone, that means he passed away?"

Her mother picked at her salad, and nodded, yes.

"How serious was it? Or were you just friends?"

"It was complicated. In all my years meeting and having men friends, it always got confusing once sex became part of the package. Rarely did it enhance. In fact, it usually ended things. I was hesitant to spoil such a perfect friendship. I don't think I laughed so much in my entire life before or since. But as for the sex, well, it was pretty much consuming. The closer we got, the closer we needed it to be. We both knew it couldn't last, except in here."

She placed her palm over her heart and gave Maddie one of those "I-am-Buddha-and-you're-a-devotee" stares.

"This was before you met my dad, right?"

"It was. Nearly two years."

"So what happened? Why didn't it last?"

"Because his heart wasn't his to give. I felt like a thief. But I couldn't help myself. I nearly packed up and followed him all the way across the country. And I'm so glad I didn't."

"So he was a friend of Noonan's too?"

"That's how I met him. They had served together in the Navy, and he came out to help him with a salvage. They were lucky enough to score some pretty incredible things, back before there were so many rules about what you could take and what you had to leave behind or register with the state. He was out for the summer visiting his old friend. Noonan had gotten out nearly six months before."

"You said across the country, where?"

"California. Moved back to California. Back to his wife."

"Mother!"

She shrugged, her large hoop earrings flashing in the afternoon sunlight. "Back in the day, I didn't worry too much about that. I figured if you threw your net out there and caught a fish, it was fair game. I didn't think about things so much like I do now. That's what age and making lots of mistakes will bring you. The trick is trying to stay *fresh* while you're getting *old*."

"Did you ever see him again?"

"I never did. I expected that one day he'd come walking right back through that door." She was pointing to the entrance. "And now I know that will never happen."

"He's gone on to fight battles elsewhere. Maybe someday you'll meet."

"I suppose I will. In time. I hope he was happy. I hope he had a good life. The world's a little sadder now, knowing that we won't meet again here at the beach at Treasure Island."

"So this was your house then? You stayed here to-gether?"

"No, it was always my house. But I let him stay. He could've stayed here the rest of his life. He made a good choice."

"He'd already chosen, Mother."

"Exactly. And in a strange twist of fate, he honored me by keeping his promise—to someone else. He made the right choice."

HER MOTHER'S WORDS haunted Madison on her way to the Salty Dog. As soon as she stepped inside the door, the familiar smells of cook Washington Jones' barbe-que and creole sauces, the general noise from the emergencies going on in the kitchen as if they battled demons escaping the gates of Hell, and the gentle country music playing in the background greeted her. It was going to be another big night. The liquor would be flowing and the plates would be flying, while the guests would consume obscene amounts of shellfish and fixings. There would be one or two major crises in the kitchen. Someone would be fired. Someone would quit. Several of the wait staff wouldn't show up and hoped to keep their jobs by showing up the next night.

It never changed. That was what was so special about this place. Everything happened at random, yet, they were all in the same pattern. Predictable in their unpredictability.

She even found herself whistling before the guitar man snuck up on her and scrambled her brain with a, "Good evening, sweetheart," whispered so close to her left ear that she could feel his hot breath on her cheek.

There he was again and she was still as breathless as the first time she saw him. Maybe it was her female alarm clock going off, her need growing so huge she didn't care about the fact that he probably slept his way up and down the Florida coast and wouldn't remember her name in the morning.

But that didn't matter. Not right now.

"Garrison Cramer, if you aren't the original Salty Dog. Just look what the sea breeze blew in tonight."

"Am I forgiven?"

"Were you bad?"

His eyes twinkled when he smiled. "I was. I was very bad. You would have been proud of me."

She felt her cheeks flush, even though threesomes

had never been anything she'd ever been interested in. But her mind was overloaded with the images, and she felt her panties go wet.

"You must lead a charmed life, Garrison."

"I am. I am blessed." He stepped closer. "So am I forgiven?"

"Let's just wait and see, shall we? What happens when your groupies show up again?"

"Oh, I don't think that will happen. They've probably moved on."

She found the opportunity to stick it to him good, at last. "Then, Garrison Cramer, you weren't bad enough. I'm going to guess they'll want a three-pete."

"Most the time, I prefer the company of just one good woman." He winked and left her soaked with sweat and gasping hard to catch her breath. It was hot enough to rival anything cook Jones could stir up.

During one of his breaks, the handsome singer asked her for a dance, and she dutifully accepted. Their foreplay—rocking back and forth to a tune not quite a slow dance, facing each other, then him spooning behind her as their hips swung in tandem—gave a healthy boost to her libido, not to mention respect from every other woman in the bar. He was a smooth dancer, he led well, and, just like Mr. James Bond, she could tell what it would feel like to wake up in his arms in the morning.

If it all went right tonight.

But it didn't. Just before midnight, a married couple got into a fight. She slapped her husband across the face, and he was preparing to retaliate when several men at the bar jumped him. The guitar man jumped in too.

In the tussle of bodies, Garrison Cramer got a belt to the nose and left with blood streaming down the front of his shirt, racing out the door on his way to the Urgent Care center.

CHAPTER 9

NED SILVER WATCHED the blue waters beneath him as his plane cruised in to land at Tampa Airport. It was a cloudless day, one of those clear ones he still loved about San Diego and Southern California. But the turquoise waters of the Florida coast were spectacular. He'd already flown over so much white beach his eyes almost hurt from the brightness.

He was excited about the new adventure coming up, the chance to do a pleasure dive and not something ordered by the military. Not that he minded that, either, but this was a different kind of excitement.

It was like how he felt going across the Pacific Ocean on an aircraft carrier once, standing with hundreds of other men looking out to the horizon in search of land. He understood how some of the early sea captains must have felt racing out into the middle of the big blue waters of the world, in search of adventure, whatever was out there. It was an urge as old as mankind itself, something he shared with every other person who felt the power of the ocean in comparison to the relative little power of his own body. The meeting between air and sea satisfied something deep inside him.

He exited the plane, walking through the lobby filled with families greeting their loved ones. The aloha shirts and different languages than he was used to in San Diego, reminded him of some of the Caribbean places he'd been to.

On his way to baggage claim, one crusty character stood out. It had to have been his dad's former Navy buddy, Noonan LaFontaine. The guy had wiry salt-and-pepper hair that sprouted every which way like dead grey straw, as if the wind was blowing through the airport. He sported a black patch over one eye, and he had a three-day stubble. He could've been a character actor in a pirate movie. He had everything but the parrot and the peg leg.

"You got to be Jake's kid. There's no doubt about it," Noonan said as he embraced him in a bear hug. With his hands gripping the tops of his arms, clearly five inches shorter than Ned, the pirate shook him and said, "You're just like how I pictured. The spitting image of your dad. I think he didn't die at all. I think you're just some kind of a trans-portal guy, you know? Like in those science-fiction films?"

Ned wanted him to release his hands but there was something about Noonan that he tolerated over any other man who would try to touch him.

"I've been told that a time or two, mostly by my mom." He stepped back. "You do know most of my dad's friends are dead?"

"So are mine. That's why I hang with the younger crowd." Noonan shrugged.

Ned adjusted his weight, pulling his laptop case over his right shoulder, and left the pirate to walk toward the baggage carousel. Noonan ran after him, laughing up a storm, waving to people he saw and thought he knew, and generally making a small spectacle of himself. Ned held his breath and wasn't sure this was the kind of vibe he was looking for in a boat captain. Although this was going to be a pleasure dive, there were always risks involved.

Ned's duffel bag was one of the first to come off the carousel. Noonan tried to grab it, but Ned shoved the computer case in his chest instead. "I'll take it, Gramps."

Noonan howled and slapped his knee over that one. It was only barely after one o'clock, but the pirate already smelled of alcohol. It was, as would have been his father's scent, the unmistakable Eau De Beer.

On the way out through the revolving doors, Noonan directed him to the short-term parking lot.

"I'm so happy you decided to come, Neddie."

Ned stopped, squared him up, and drilled a look that didn't require words, but he spoke anyway. "For the record, Gramps or Noonan or whatever you want me to call you, the name is Ned. I haven't been Neddie since I was six years old. I hated it then, and I hate it worse now. So if you don't want me to turn around and catch a plane back to California, you better not call me that again. Agreed?"

"I don't have a problem with that. I was just being…"

"You were being an asshole, like my dad. If you stop being an asshole, we'll get along just fine. You have to know that my dad and I were never close, so if you're thinking you're going to take his spot or be just like him, and that's gonna make me feel real comfortable or good, you've got shit for brains. So let's just get that straight out and on the table right now okay?"

"You don't have to say it twice, Son. I know all about your dad." His bloodshot eye nearly teared up when he finished his thought. "I know your dad better than you do."

The man turned and made a beeline for the parking lot. Ned's long legs kept pace with the pirate, but he had to work at it to do so.

They jumped into a light turquoise pickup truck with the Barry Bones logo on the side, depicting a patched pirate face missing several prominent teeth, grinning wide, sporting an earring and wearing a red bandanna. Noonan could've posed for the picture except for the teeth.

Ned strapped in after loading his duffel in the back. He held his laptop on his knees. Noonan jumped in and avoided his seatbelt.

Ned watched the blue waters on either side of a large arched bridge leading from the highway system outside of Tampa over to the gulf beaches. He'd never seen so many boats in one place before. Houses along the shore all had docks, and many also had swimming pools, something he didn't see in San Diego much. The weather was perfect, similar to San Diego but warmer. In the distance, he could see the ocean.

"I was thinking I'd bring you by that little place I found, get your gear dropped off, and we could go grab something to eat if you're up to it.

"I could do something to eat."

"If you don't like what I got for you, just stay put for a couple of days, see if it wears on you. I managed to get it for free, so you won't have to pay me or anybody else back, okay?"

"Geez, thank you. How'd you arrange that?"

Noonan grinned. "I don't have a lot of money, but I do have friends. At my age, kid, friends are everything."

"I haven't been to this side of Florida before. It's nice," Ned muttered.

"I've spent most of my time on the other coast, to be honest. But I love the gulf side much better. Warmer, I think, more temperate. And it's slower. I mean, we got lots of tourism here, no question about it. But it's happier. You know what I mean?"

Ned stared straight ahead as the bridge dead-ended into a small two-lane boulevard, heading north and south along the beach.

"This here is Gulf Boulevard, for obvious reasons. You have your beachside properties, and then you have your inland properties, which sometimes are on a waterway. In any direction, you're no more than five or six blocks from some body of water. I think that's why I like it"

Noonan turned right and headed north. Ned saw glimpses of turquoise water and white beaches in between two-story rental units and occasionally a large condo complex. Along the way, it was dotted with beach shops and rental agencies, renting everything from vacation cabins to surfboards, golf carts, and beach bicycles. He passed a lot of ice cream stores. There were shops on both sides of the road selling fishing and beach gear, flip-flops, bathing suits, tanning lotion, and a couple of *taquerias* with open air *palapas* just like Ned had seen in Mexico. There were lots of fish and chips places and a smattering of outdoor bars with brightly-colored umbrellas. Occasionally, they had to stop between lights to allow couples or families to cross the road, usually towing a canvas wagon filled with towels and equipment.

They also passed several groups of walkers and occasionally a tandem bicycle. Ned felt himself starting to relax, even though Noonan was quick to hit on the gas and slow to hit the brakes.

"See? Nothing fancy, but not too shabby, either."

They turned left down a paved road that ended at the edge of a wooden bridge over the sand dunes. It was the Treasure Island beach access trail. Off to the side was an alleyway, unpaved, just wide enough to accommodate two cars passing. On both sides of the path were smaller shacks, some of them well-painted and others left to the sea's devices. Vacation rental signs hung in most of the yards or attached to the upper eaves of the houses, colorfully lettered in bright Caribbean paint, with names like Pete's Paradise and Laura's Lair. Pictures of fish, starfish, and mermaids adorned fences and sides of buildings. Noonan pulled into the driveway of a tiny pink house that sat right on the beach.

"It isn't much, I warn you. This place is going to get torn down, and the owner has plans to build a McMansion sort of triplex building. He wants to live upstairs and rent out down below. But for now, this place is vacant, and it has a little bit of furniture. I hope you like it. And the price is right," he reminded as he exited the truck.

Ned ran right behind the pirate, his canvas slip-ons crunching on the white mixture of crushed shells and stones. Noonan produced a set of keys and unlocked the front door, which was slightly warped, causing Noonan to have to lean into it hard with his shoulder. At the second try, it gave way and let them enter, but part of the door trim had cracked.

Inside, the house smelled of mildew, but Ned thought it was nothing that a few open windows wouldn't take care of. It hadn't been updated in many years. That surprised him, because Ned thought all these beach properties saw themselves underwater every few years due to the storms. But this one looked like it had survived many seasons of Winters and lots of Fall hurricanes.

"Home sweet home, kid."

"It's funky. I like it." Ned walked through the doorway into a small bedroom, which barely had room for the king-sized bed. He'd been dreading to discover a lumpy full-sized mattress so was thrilled with the king.

He threw his duffel bag on the bed, unzipped it, and hung up a jacket and two shirts he brought.

Noonan was watching him, leaning into the doorway.

"Don't know if you smoke, but they'll allow it, too."

"I'm not a smoker."

"Good to see you're prepared," Noonan nodded at the shirts Ned was hanging up.

"I thought I should bring something for at least one night out. Do you have any plans for that?"

"Let's see what kind of luck we have first. Good idea though. You never know what the sea is going to bring you. It could be cause for celebration."

"I don't care about what the sea brings me, as long as the restaurant doesn't refuse to serve me."

"You're a very astute traveler. I'm not gonna take you anywhere a pair of khakis and a T-shirt wouldn't do. But it's good to be prepared."

Noonan returned to the living room. "This is always how I judge the bones of a house. I like to be just outside the sand bar like this one is. I like to be able to see the water, have my coffee out on my private beach, or sit out at night under the stars. This one has a fire pit too. Nobody will bother you here. Everybody who lives on the street is from somewhere else. Some people live here, some people are running away, and some people just don't know what the fuck they're doing."

Ned found himself chuckling. The pirate was easy to like. Maybe it was the smell of the ocean or just the fact that the damned view was stunningly beautiful, but

Ned knew he was going to be okay. And Noonan understood Ned needed some alone time. There would be no father-son play acting here, and the old captain would be a good resource so Ned could explore this area more.

"If you want to get a car, you'd have to go into Largo or someplace. I should've asked you at the airport. The cars are a little expensive. You can get along just fine here in a golf cart. And where we're going to be is just down the road a bit. I got the Bones all fueled up and ready to go."

Ned shook his head. "I don't think I want to rent a vehicle but will play it by ear. Only thing I want is to get some groceries. Do you have time to run me down to someplace I can fill up my fridge?"

"Of course. Let's go do that now, and then we can head over for a late lunch/early dinner. I've got some people I want to introduce you to."

Ned purchased staples he was going to need, going off the list he made before he left. They stowed everything away, chilled the beers, and were ready to go.

He discovered his stomach had been doing flip-flops. The small breakfast he'd been served on the plane wasn't quite enough to keep him going. He was itching to have some fresh seafood.

Noonan hit Gulf Boulevard one more time, and was pointing out various bars, restaurants, and places of interest. He showed him where the best place to buy wine was, and where not to buy a rubbery pizza. He recommended a little Mexican place within walking distance of Ned's new cottage and told him to avoid the tandoori restaurant next-door.

They pulled up to another bar restaurant combination with an outdoor patio sprinkled under colorful beach umbrellas. Even at three o'clock in the afternoon, there were a good number of cars in the parking lot.

Ned waited for his eyes to adjust to the darkness. The food smelled great. Noonan was dragging him over to sit on a stool at a huge U-shaped bar. The shapely female bartender was leaning over to stock beer bottles in a refrigerator, and it was hard to miss how perfect her ass was. Not that he was looking.

But when she stood, her shoulders and back were covered in bright white-blonde ringlets of spun gold, reaching down all the way past her waist. She was tall, her arms well-tanned, but when she turned to face him, her blue eyes flashed, and then she looked away. He couldn't take his eyes off of her. She was some kind of angel, her face beautiful without the aid of any makeup that he could detect.

She chanced another look at him, and he felt a warm ripple wash all over him again. Whoever she was, he was sure he'd never met anyone like her before.

"Madison!" Noonan was calling to her.

She approached almost timidly, except he sensed she was far from timid. Her gentle scent wafted towards him, and he felt completely enthralled, enchanted. He was laid out bare and could not stop staring.

"This here's my buddy's son, Ned Silver." He leaned over the counter. "He's a Navy SEAL, but shhh! We don't tell anyone."

Ned was irritated. "Come on, Noonan. You know that's not cool."

The girl's eyes were all over him. He felt he might blush. "Your secret's safe with me," she whispered, holding out her hand. "I'm Madison."

She gave a firm handshake. Her palm was warm and as sweaty as his was. "Nice to meet you, Madison. I'm Ned."

"He told me that already," she said as they continued shaking hands. She smirked and withdrew her paw because he wasn't going to let it go.

"She's part of the crew, Ned. She's done lots of underwater film work." Ned glanced up at her. "Tell him about that James Bond film you were in."

"Thunder Dive," she said. The dimple at the side of her mouth formed and then disappeared. "I did the body double for the bad girl." She watched his reaction like it was important to her.

"I saw that movie. I liked it. I thought they filmed that in the Caribbean."

"Nope, right out here." She angled her head back to point to the beach.

"How'd you get that job?"

Noonan inserted himself. "Are you crazy, Ned? Look at her!"

I am, dammit. I'm just trying to talk for Chrissakes!

"I did some water skiing shows at SeaWorld a few years ago, and some underwater film photography, and, well, I don't know if they even auditioned anyone else. I just got the job."

She had a nice shrug too. He was going to have to stop staring or he'd be drooling soon.

"So you like to dive then?" He didn't like how it sounded.

"I do. I even go deep. Mostly for pleasure. There's not a lot of work out here now, unless you want to help raise an oil platform." Her big blue eyes rolled, and she twisted her upper lip.

The air was thick between them. Noonan was chuckling under his breath. Ned licked his lips. His mouth was parched.

Someone called Madison's name, and she excused herself.

In her wake, Ned's insides were all jumbled up, yet he didn't have the desire to get everything straight. His heart raced. Expectation zoomed and made fun of his ordered life with everything put in its proper place. Logic was disappearing. Teetering out of control, he felt like he'd been hit by a tsunami.

And he loved it.

CHAPTER 10

MADISON COULD FEEL his eyes on her behind. Although she didn't mind the attention, she'd already written Ned off as a lost cause. He was too young, too clean-cut, didn't display enough flawed behavior or personality. And he certainly didn't need her brand of healing.

As she waited on tables, she scratched her head several times and asked for customers to repeat the order. She was distracted by her thoughts, not really thinking about him as a potential partner—she just couldn't stop thinking about him period.

Besides, soon Garrison was going to be sauntering in, no doubt needing an evening of commiseration. She had visions of being extremely careful as she kissed him, avoiding his poor nose. That's what she had in mind. She had no appetite for picking up a youngster.

But every time she turned, every time she looked over her shoulder to make sure someone was tending the bar, every time she heard old Noonan laughing or hit the wooden countertop with his fist, attention always drifted off toward the newcomer. The most irritating thing about it was that he didn't seem to mind the attention, either.

When Garrison Cramer finally darkened the doorway, swinging his guitar case over his shoulder, he gave her a wink and a puppy dog smile. One of his eyes had a deep purple ring beneath it. His nose was red, and there was a surgical strip covering a tiny cut above the bridge of his nose. He was a tall, dark, and dangerous piece of maleness in need of all the things Madison loved to dish out.

"Am I forgiven?" He stepped so close she could feel the heat of his thigh against her without them touching.

"THAT DEPENDS ON how bad you were." She stared back up to him, unafraid, enjoying the scent of his being. He was a land lover, no question about it, and she was queen of the ocean. There were lots of interesting contrasts and other things they could explore together.

"Now as for being bad, that's where you come in, Madison."

Her spine tingled in such a good way. She looked down at her feet, inhaled, and smiled to herself. If they were alone, he would've brought those big arms around her waist and plastered her with a kiss so deep she knew she would be hooked. But in public, all she could do was feel the tension in his chest. His breathing sounded like the roar of the ocean.

And all the better, college kid, clean-cut Navy seal Ned fucking Silver was watching the whole thing. She hoped he took it as a warning that she would not be easy to charm.

"So is that a yes?"

"Right now,"—she looked deep into his eyes—"I'm having the time of my life just having you wonder about that. But I would say, the odds are definitely in your favor."

"Then I better get set up, right? And would you do me the honor of accepting a dance with me sometime tonight?"

"I'd like that, Garrison. I'd like that a lot."

She watched him walk away, enter the patio area, greet several people casually, remove his guitar and set up his stool and equipment.

Madison made the mistake of noticing the perch next to Noonan was vacant. Half a beer was left on the counter, as well as an unfinished crab salad. She approached the pirate.

"You get stood up already?"

"No, he saw some people he knew from San Diego

or Norfolk." Noonan pointed to an area across the patio where Ned was seated with his back to her, talking to two other clean-cut, muscled, and overly tattooed guys. He rubbed the bridge of his nose. "You and the crooner an item? Isn't he a little old, worn off parts around the edges a bit?" Noonan quizzed.

Madison slapped him with the end of her bar rag. "I like his voice, and I like it that the only strings that come with him are the ones on his guitar."

"You are so much like your mother. Does she know you do this, pick up guys at work?"

She gawked back at Noonan. "This is work?"

Iris was making drinks behind the bar. Madison asked her to go wait on Ned and his friends.

"I can't. I got my hands full here. I've got an order of ten."

Madison took her tray, pulled her order chits from the back pocket of her jeans, and crossed the patio to serve them.

Ned gave her a warm smile. "Madison, these are some of my friends." To the group, he explained, "Madison's gonna work on the dive I've been hired for."

"Nice to meet you," said one of the SEALs. "I'm Andy." He extended his hand.

Madison jammed the tray into her chest, put the notebook in her left, and shook his hand as well as the young sailor's across the table from him, who said his name was Reed.

"So I'm going to guess you guys also fish together?"

They all chuckled. "Yes, ma'am," came the answer in unison.

"Madison here's some movie star. Got to be a Bond Girl, isn't that right?" Ned informed them.

She was thinking about all the fun things she had done on that shoot, which made her blush but kept her lips sealed.

"Really?" asked one of the gentlemen.

"I've done a few things. Most of them I'm proud of." She gave them a winning smile. It was her job to keep the customers happy, after all. Besides, Boy Scouts like these were good for business. "Now, what can I get you?"

Before they began ordering, Madison heard the syrupy sweet voice of Garrison Cramer. "Ladies and gentlemen, I just wanted to dedicate my first song to the most beautiful woman in this whole place. Miss Madison? Would you take a bow please?"

Her cheeks flamed instantly as all eyes quickly turned in her direction. She gave a delicate bow then blew Cramer a kiss and got a standing ovation.

She focused her attention back on her three SEAL customers. Brushing the hair from her forehead, she used her little notebook to fan herself. "Well, that was unexpected." In the background, she heard Garrison Cramer singing a beautiful love song.

That raised Ned's eyebrows. "Well, I was going to ask you for a ride home later on, but I can see you're otherwise occupied."

"Really? You think?"

"Yes, I think he has plans for you tonight, and God knows I wouldn't want to impose. I am looking to make friends since we're gonna be working together. I don't know this area at all, and I don't have a car. I'm sure I'll work it out, somehow."

One of the SEALs offered, and Madison couldn't miss Ned's stern response, shutting the man down.

"You always have Noonan," Madison pointed out. She observed the pirate sitting alone, waiting. She felt a little sorry for him.

"Yup. And speaking of the man, I should get back over to him. I'll catch you guys tomorrow night?"

"Sure thing. We don't go back till next weekend. Shoot, I like the scenery here so much I might never go back to Little Creek," said Andy.

Ned stood, brushing past her, emanating a little grumble as he did so. Removing a twenty from his wallet, he placed it on Madison's tray. "I've got their first round, okay?"

"Got it." She stared up at him and caught a wink.

"I hope you don't mind, I was messin' with you a

little bit. Just a little good, clean fun."

That's when she realized he wasn't going to be easy to get rid of. And he was a whole lot smarter and probably more experienced than she thought he was.

ABOUT AN HOUR later, Madison nearly ran into Ned rounding the corner from the kitchen.

"I'm about to take off. Can I ask you for a dance, sort of give the singing cowboy some competition?"

"I'm kind of busy. I'll take a raincheck." It was what she had to say to stay in control.

"It might increase his ardor, could be real good for you," he suggested, giving her a wink.

"Like he needed it," she teased in return.

Ned shrugged. "If you say so. I would have thought you'd have gone for someone who wasn't so long in the tooth and didn't lust after anyone in a skirt. He's kind of obvious, don't you think? But you know what they say, whatever *floats your boat*."

He had just made fun of her in the most gentlemanly manner, catching her off guard.

"And how would you know what sort of man I like to play with?"

"Oh, it's play, is it? Well then, darlin', I'm out."

"I meant that in rhetorical terms," she protested. "I meant—"

"Sure. It is a big game for you, isn't it? You like to

be in control, because that makes the man need to be stronger, right? Have you ever just let a nice, smooth man take his time, and rock your world, and you didn't have to do a thing?"

That was unexpected. Madison thought she should be offended. "Supposed to be fifty-fifty, doesn't it?"

"Only if you don't trust the one in control. How nice would that be to anticipate, but not know, except to recognize that you don't have to lift a finger and you let him do all the lovin' and you get to do all the enjoyin'? Think about it."

He turned on his heel. She had turned down the dance, after all, so there wasn't anything left to be said. But it pissed her off to see him clear the doorway and disappear into the night air. Noonan wasn't anywhere to be found, either.

The singing cowboy acted like he never saw a thing. Except he suddenly looked like second place to Madison.

CHAPTER 11

NED WENT FOR a barefoot run on the beach just before the sun rose. He did thirty pushups and a couple dozen sit ups. With his ankles caressed by the surf, he stretched, rotating his arms and doing neck curls in both directions. Satisfied he'd continued his routine on the first morning in a new location, just like he'd been trained, he surveyed his surroundings.

Take care of your body and your mind, and everything else works out.

By the time the grey pink sky turned into a full-blown rose orange, several other runners and bicyclists had joined him. A group of older women walked briskly past him, several of them waving.

Today, they'd start the dive.

Ned thought he would sleep well last night, but he wound up tossing about. He finally changed the sheets, putting the others in the wash. The lull of the machine whir was the last thing he heard before crashing. He couldn't remember the dream he had, but they had been vivid and filled with bright color.

He made coffee and had a bowl of granola with a banana. He checked his computer for news from base. On his cell, the informal group chat he had with several of the Team guys had deteriorated last night into nonsense. Someone posted a picture he shouldn't and asked that everyone erase it, which Ned did. He was glad he missed the drama of the night with a bunch of horny single guys trying to…do what? Live a normal life? It was far from normal. Waiting wasn't normal. Recovering after a deployment wasn't normal. There was still all the shit going on at home with their community, family, and their uncertain future. As much as they tried to be a force for good, there was still the realization after they came home that nothing really ever changed.

The news was the same. Someone got hurt in a training accident. One of their old instructors was retiring, and a party was planned. Someone else was getting married and another party was planned at the Brownlees, their official Team party after the deployment and the debriefing. He was sorry to miss that one. He liked Coop's in-laws. Coop was a regular stand-up guy too. Both he and Kyle had always treated Ned with respect.

He finished his breakfast then made a peanut butter and jelly sandwich and wrapped it in plastic. He brought two bottles of water and two apples, placing everything in a gallon plastic bag, sticking it in his slender dive backpack along with an extra pair of trunks and T-shirt and some heavy-duty sunscreen and bug repellant. Under his khakis he wore trunks. Hoisting the backpack over his shoulder, he stepped into his canvas slip-ons and walked out to the alleyway and then to Gulf Boulevard. He'd driven past the dock last night and knew it would be just a short walk.

Noonan kept the Barry Bones at a sport fishing club berth, although he wasn't a paying member. Ned was told the private clubhouse was a popular meeting place for boats taking tourists fishing out on the bay, and the Bones was one of the most requested dive boats. Although not as many shipwrecks as on the Atlantic side, there were still a fair number of good sites for novice divers to check out. Noonan told him he was known to bring back everyone safely, albeit a little drunk.

He wasn't like any of the big party boats with scores of partygoers who practically had to be lifted off when they came back to dock. Those black pirate ships blasted music and poured booze to excess, feigning to terrorize the quiet beachgoers on the shore. Their Hollywood-style swashbuckling was ridiculous but entertaining for many of the college and younger honeymooners who knew nothing about pirates, boats, or diving. Ned had seen real pirates, and those guys were definitely not funny.

Noonan had piles of wet suits and equipment laid out for his three divers. He pointed to Ned's pile. "Check them out for me, will you? That suit's about your size. Might be a little big."

Ned held up the shortie, the preferred choice for warm water dives, cutting off just above the elbows and above the knees. It was intact but had definitely seen better days. He checked the gauges and connections on the tanks and tried on the one-piece headgear with the built-in com.

"Do we each have a spare?" Ned asked.

Noonan gave him the thumbs-up, pointing to four tanks secured in a stand on board. Ned took his equipment and stepped off the pier and onto the boat. Below deck, were two bedrooms—one was probably Noonan's with an oversized bed no larger than a single on land. The other room had four bunks, no wider than a double ironing board, but otherwise spacious and adequate. He knew that's where the three of them would sleep, if the dive required they stay overnight on the gulf.

The galley kitchen had a big stainless steel sink, a microwave and built-in coffee maker, and a one-burner propane cooktop. A small stainless fridge was secured underneath the countertop. Beyond was the head with shower. He stowed his pack, setting it on a lower bunk, and poured himself a mug of coffee, climbing back up to see if he could help Noonan with anything.

"No, I think I got everything. I got a fridge down there if you need to keep anything cold, and sorry, I was going to get donuts but never left the ship."

"No worries, Noonan. I'm good. Hope you got beer for the return trip."

"That I do," Noonan said as he organized ties, buoys and ropes, placing them in several plastic containers smelling of fish and probably used for storing fresh catch. Ned figured the empty large blue container with a drain in it at the stern near one of the outboards was for placing things they found on the dive.

"What time are the others coming?"

"Madison's usually early. But I said eight o'clock." Noonan checked his watch, "Anytime now."

Ned saw Madison's shapely form in her dark turquoise suit, carrying a pair of bright pink flippers. She'd also brought snorkel gear which Ned found amusing. She gave him a big smile and waved.

"Hey, Noonan, how deep are we going?" Ned thought perhaps he'd misunderstood.

"Less than a hundred, maybe eighty, how I pegged

it. I was out there two days ago and located it with sonar, marked it with a buoy."

"Morning," Madison said to him. Her fresh face was more exposed now that all that blonde hair was tied back in two long braids she lashed together with hot pink bands. She could have made a beautiful Viking princess in a movie shoot, if they wore wetsuits.

"You have a nice night?"

She wrinkled up her nose.

"I warned you about the cowboy."

It was nice to see her laugh. "He's not a cowboy."

"And?"

"He's a good dancer."

"And?" He was enjoying the tease. He also noted she wasn't as frosty as she'd been last night, which meant one of two things, and both of them were sending visions to his head that were damned distracting.

She shrugged. "I'm not used to waiting in line. And that's all I'm going to tell you!"

Well, good for you. He'd been right about her.

She filed past him, greeted Noonan, and examined the equipment he'd left out for her. She'd brought her own secondary tank, brightly colored in psychedelic patterns. Ned continued to sip his coffee. Noonan showed her the headpiece they would wear and demonstrated the wire for the com.

At last, the third diver, Travis Hicks, arrived, running down the dock in red flip-flops, an open palm trees shirt exposing a white hairy chest, matching red trunks, and a Yankee baseball cap worn backwards. He also wore thick glasses and would need a mask enhancement.

Shortly before nine o'clock, they took off in the forty-one foot Barry Bones, headed due West. Ned deposited his mug in the galley downstairs and then took a seat up front next to Madison, avoiding the loud twin diesels at the rear. Travis sat next to Noonan on the bridge, watching the scanners logging the depth of the Bay. It took nearly five miles out before the floor dropped below thirty feet, and quickly, they were in much deeper waters.

Nearly an hour after leaving shore, they came upon a red buoy bobbing in the relatively calm blue waters of the Gulf. Noonan dropped anchor and turned off the engines well in advance of the marker. He had been showing Travis the debris field ahead that led to the barge they were going to explore.

"You're going to have to swim in a ways to get to the main hull. I didn't want to disturb it when we dropped anchor."

The four of them congregated in the galley table so Noonan could share the pictures he'd brought.

"Here's what the barge looked like new. The *Regina*

Cubana. It slept nearly twenty-five men, and had a regular run all over the Cuban and Florida coastline. But who we're looking for is Otis. He was the cook's dog. That mutt had traveled all over the Caribbean, but they lived in Cuba, and that's where the cook signed on. Never traveled without the dog."

"You said it was the dog's collar we're after?" asked Ned.

"Yes, and I have a picture of it." Noonan scrambled through a folder of maps and pictures, magazine clippings. He pulled out a drawing of a necklace around the neck of a pretty island girl. It appeared to have jewels encrusted around the choker with a cross dangling in the center.

"That's no dog collar," gasped Madison.

"No, it's not. And apparently, the gems are nearly worthless, except that they are old and have history. It was a piece of costume jewelry created for the governor's wife to wear when she was out in the countryside. It was a replica of the real thing that is in a British maritime museum in Antigua. Story has it that this was the mistress' slave girl, and when the woman died, she left her the fake. The family, of course, inherited the real one. She was our cook's wife, but not for very long. When she passed, our man took to the sea with his favorite mutt, Otis, who didn't mind wearing this thing around his neck on all the voyages he went on. This dog and the collar were considered to be good luck to the men who worked the barge."

"How will we find something like that?"

"It's platinum and probably glass, if any of it remains. Our metal detector will pick up whatever's left. Of course, it will look like a pile of rocks," said Noonan. "It won't resemble anything in this picture. You'll have to use your imagination. Two hundred years under water does things. It will be full encased in hardened rock and coral."

"Were they hauling anything valuable?" asked Travis.

"Probably not, at least not what was listed on the manifest. There were three survivors who managed to escape in a small rowboat, who told the stories."

"Who hired you?" asked Ned.

"A family in North Carolina traced their ancestry to this woman, the former slave girl, and got permission to petition the estate for our dive. They want the collar. It's worthless other than the sentimental value of it. And we're given some rights to items we find worth less than five hundred dollars, but everything has to be catalogued first. And no human remains, no bones or anything that would destroy their graves. Understood?"

"After all these years, you won't find any remains," said Ned.

Noonan chuckled. "Depends on what fell on top of them. I've seen some things that would scare the liver out of you. Bodies floating to the surface after several hundred years under water, if the conditions of the wreck are right. They just melt into the sea by the time they get close to the surface. Really weird stuff."

Madison had a disgusted look on her face.

"Most of what was being transported when the freak hurricane hit was perishable: Grain, molasses, honey, and some lumber from Cuba on its way to up near the panhandle. It was a little too far offshore for most those who survived the sinking to be able to swim to safety, unfortunately."

"Did they carry passengers?" asked Travis.

"Not listed. But back then, there were always stow-aways. This was fifty years before the Civil War, the slave trade was still going strong, but there were runaways. Who knows who could have been on board? The accommodations would not be very deluxe, even for the captain."

Travis and Ned suited up as Noonan helped Madison with her equipment. She strapped her extra tank to a belt around her waist. Noonan asked Travis to man the metal detector. All three of them tested the battery-operated com system and would do so again once in the water. They would be going with a long dive line so Noonan could signal them if he needed them to surface. The Bones didn't have anything more sophisticated than that. There wouldn't be any small submersibles sending pictures up top.

Ned followed Madison and Travis into the water. They adjusted their face masks and tested the com, gave the thumbs-up to Noonan, and, one by one, descended into the warm water of the Gulf and into the deep.

Madison's bright pink fins were easy to spot, her long legs slowly pedaling her forward and down into the darker water. Lack of silt made everything clear, sending down shards of light from the surface. Varieties of colorful small fish curiously hung around them. He could see several sparkling particles floating, catching the sun's rays before they descended further. The temperature of the water was much cooler, but still not as cold as he expected.

The image of Madison's shapely form was something Ned liked watching as they continued their descent. He was hopeful for what lay below and the promise of recovering objects long lost. He savored the recreational aspect of their adventure. No bad guys coming after them. No worries about being detected or having a malfunction with their rebreathers. It was just a pleasurable journey into the unknown with someone who was also an unknown factor in his life.

Of all the things he thought he would be doing, this

wasn't one of them. He was following a mermaid in a turquoise wetsuit with pink fins. But, unlike his father, he was going on a treasure dive.

For a dog collar.

CHAPTER 12

TRAVIS REACHED THE floor first and began swishing the lighted detector over the debris field as Madison and Ned caught up to him. She knew from prior salvage dives that often the more experienced divers were the first to get down to a site, looking for the easy finds. This was different. It was going to have to be a meticulous combing of the area, identifying the spots they'd come back to and inspect further. Sort of like an archeological survey. She'd brought her waterproof camera and started taking pictures of areas Travis lingered on.

He found some tracings and pointed down to several mounds of reddish-brown rocks less than a foot tall. Madison shot several photos of the area and moved on.

Ned's flashlight was wider and threw out more light than the ones Travis and Madison had. She gave him a thumbs-up when he located what appeared to be a hole several feet deep and about twenty feet wide. It looked like a crater of some kind.

She dove in after Ned and took pictures. The sides of the crater looked like the frayed edges of a basket. Pieces of metal and crusted timbers long gone lay strewn around the floor. Madison catalogued everywhere Ned illuminated. She stayed close by his side.

"What do you think made this?" she asked into the com.

"Looks like a blast to me. Not sure if it was something dropped from the surface or internal, but it looks more recent than the wreck itself, if that's what we've found."

She nodded her head.

"Hey, guys, we definitely need to get back here," they heard Travis call out.

Travis was hovering over a debris field that mounted up nearly twenty feet. At the ocean floor, they found the remnants of a ship's anchor that was protruding from the sand nearly three feet, with a point fashioned at the end of the curved tip. Next to it was a concreted tube, appearing to be part of a cannon, also buried in the sand floor.

"That definitely didn't come from a barge," said Ned.

"Neither of them did. That's the shape of some of the galleon's anchors I've seen," said Travis.

The two objects were firmly planted in the seabed and did not budge.

"Noonan's going to have kittens over these. Make sure you get some great shots, Maddie," said Travis.

"Go check out that crater behind us, Travis. Tell me what you think," asked Ned.

On his way past them, Madison heard Travis say, "Make sure you take pictures of that wall of debris, Madison. See if you can find an inscription on either piece. Noonan is going to blow his mind when he sees this."

"I'm on it." She dove closer. Ned's light made a wide arc as her hands smoothed over the pitted surface of the cannon. She spotted a reddish pile knee-high to one side. She asked for light, then took pictures of all of it.

"You see anything?" Ned asked.

"No, but Noonan will look these up. I don't think he expected our barge to be anywhere close to another ship. Maybe it crashed on top of it."

"And that pile looks like cannonballs."

"I was thinking the same thing. Red means iron, right?" she asked.

"Yup. Noonan said a year later someone came in to recover what they could from the barge. They would have seen this stuff too. It must have moved during storm seasons."

"It does look like something had been dragged through this area. See the shape?"

She pointed out to him.

Ned nodded, giving her another thumbs-up.

"Let's look at the cannon," Madison said as they heard Travis behind them.

"Hey, guys, you got pictures of the insides of that thing?" he asked, meaning the crater.

Madison nodded.

"That's not a blast. That's a salvage suck. Somebody's been working on this site, or tried to. Some of these commercial salvage operations use those power vacuums. I think that's what was started there."

"You see anything small enough we can bring to the surface?" asked Ned.

"I wanna come back down with the nets," said Travis. "Over there, I picked up metal. You could bring up one or two of those smaller stones, and we can have a look."

Madison tried to pry loose a couple of the tiny mounds no larger than the size of an orange, choosing the darker colored ones, but couldn't dislodge it. Ned assisted with his knife until they broke one free. He pointed to the surface, and everyone nodded agreement. They tugged on the dive line three times, indicating they were ascending. Noonan tugged back his acknowledgement.

Slowly, the three of them ascended, taking turns to examine the small rock. Madison carefully peeled off soft debris then handed it back to Travis.

"You want to be careful, Maddie. Some of these attached sea skeletons can be sharp," Ned informed her.

In their hand-over hand maneuvers up the line, her arm got hooked inside Ned's left. One of his hands accidentally brushed her backside. One pink fin swished the side of his thigh. She felt his hand on the back of her waist when they neared the surface. The gesture was more than telling her she could go up first.

As she reached the ladder, Ned began removing her fins, one by one, his gentle fingers gliding around and under her heel to release her foot from the plastic form. He was careful, measured, and very, very slow, much slower than he needed to be, going out of his way not to cause her any pain or discomfort at all. With her heart racing, she watched his dedication to her safety and noted his huge hands tenderly gripping her ankle. When he was done, he looked up at her and gave her feet a squeeze. He tucked the fins beneath his arm and then removed his own and climbed the ladder behind her.

Up top, Travis was describing to Noonan what they'd seen. Madison was barely paying attention. She felt her backside warmed by the heat of a very powerful man standing behind her, barely touching, but pressing a towel to her neck and shoulders. She unzipped the front of her suit several inches, as if needing to breathe. Ned's hand grazed her hip as he turned over control of the towel to her, squeezing her shoulder through the cotton. He set down the fins and pulled off his face-mask.

Still with her back turned to him, she had difficulty removing her mask. Part of her braid on one side had gotten entangled in the rubberized collar. Ned's fingers slid up her neck, pulling the material away from her skin, stretching it and pulling it off her skull smoothly until she was free.

She turned to say thank you, but he'd already start-ed hosing off both their masks and fins with fresh water. His suit was unzipped nearly to his waist. His rippled abs were difficult not to notice. When he peeled down the upper layer of the suit, his huge bare shoulders dwarfed her. His sculpted and tanned torso took her breath away as she followed the lines of his magnificent body to where the suit remained just below his waist.

She put the towel to her face, inhaling deeply, and then squeeze-dryed her braids one by one.

Noonan was ecstatic. "Madison! Show me the pic-tures, girl!"

Ned leaned across her, his arm touching her

frontside, picked up the camera and tossed it to the captain.

"You good?" he said as he smiled down at her. "Everything okay now?"

"Yes, thank you. I get that sometimes. So anxious to get that mask off my face, I sometimes get my hair caught."

"We wouldn't want that now, would we?" he said, his palm brushing down the braid behind her right ear.

She was putty in his hands and tried desperately not to show it.

"I think it's a panic thing." She shrugged and tried to be casual, but she knew he saw right through it.

Noonan was having kittens. "I can't believe it. Oh my God! Oh my God!" he said over and over again.

"So what do you think about the suck hole?" Travis asked him.

"That hole's at least a year old. You'd see some sharp lines in the sand if it was this season. This whole place has been rocked by the weather, most of it for decades. But I'm going to have to do a little research to make sure no one's made a claim. I don't want to get myself or the estate into trouble."

"What does that mean?" asked Ned.

"Means I have to inquire about the claims in this area. I didn't look for a salvage claim. I was mainly worried about some of this being a registered historical site, since the barge was well known and had already been salvaged and left with no value declared. But no one filed anything for it since way back in the 1880s. I'm going to have to dig around for a day and see what I can find back in Tampa."

"Can we go back down?" Travis asked.

"Let's not draw attention to it. I'm pulling the buoy, too. We don't want to say anything until I get my research done."

"Damn it," said Travis.

"And you make sure to keep your mouth shut, too, son. No barking off your mouth to any of your friends I tried to hire. Understood?"

"I got it! You can trust me!" Travis said, holding his hand over his heart.

"So now what?" Madison wanted to know. She was standing perpendicular to Ned and could still feel the warmth from his body. He could have distanced himself, sat down, or started to put away the equipment, but he remained there.

"We can grab a bite. I got some breakfast burritos I'll microwave up and let's talk. Then I'm going to head back in. You guys can stay, if you want!" Noonan said with a grin.

Everyone chuckled.

"Ned, would you wind up the dive line and Travis, will you kill that buoy?"

"Yessir," they both said.

"Madison, help me in the kitchen, would you?"

She followed Noonan down the ladder, at the last minute looking up to watch Ned winding the plastic dive line around from his elbow to up over his wrist and into his hand with the other one leading the way. He was staring right back down on her without a smile, and again, her heart raced.

The small space made it impossible not to rub up against everyone. Madison was used to this on many of the dives she'd been on, but this time, with the presence of this one big guy who she guessed was about six-five, the space seemed half the size.

As directed, she sliced fresh fruit and lay down a platter in front of Travis and Ned, who were waiting. Noonan asked her to slip in across from Ned, and he brought beers and a couple sodas, sliding in next to her. When the microwave went off, he added half a dozen breakfast burritos and a tamale, which he chose. He returned with plastic forks and paper towels.

The food was good. But distracting was the fact that her knees touched the front of Ned's, and he wasn't moving. Neither made eye contact, but from the side, she knew he was having a hard time containing a grin. The frown creasing the bridge of his nose was artificial, self-made. When he spread his knees to the sides, it allowed her more room, until he closed his legs against hers, trapping her gently. He was messing with her again. She had not picked up any of this in the brief time she'd gotten to know him.

Noonan was scanning through the pictures she'd taken. "See that?"

Travis spoke up. "We did. We're thinking iron? Like cannon balls?"

"Looks like it to me." He enlarged the picture of the anchor and then the cannon. "No forge marks?"

"I didn't find any weld marks either. Just a couple feet of it sticking out of the floor. That would give some indication of age, right?"

"A mark would be best, but based on what I've seen, the shape of this tip could have come from a smaller anchor. Sometimes the galleons had several, depending on the depth and the weather."

"This is way more exciting than a dog collar," said Travis, his mouth full of beans and eggs.

"You be sure to watch your mouth, kid. I mean it." Noonan pointed directly at the young man's nose. "I'll kick your butt if you breathe a word."

"Hey, I got it. No problem here. How long before you know?"

"That depends on what I find," Noonan blurted out.

THE RIDE BACK was longer. Noonan didn't want to

retrace his exact same course in case he was being tracked. They stopped several times for a quick swim in the warm water. Madison stripped down to the tank suit she had on under her wetsuit. It wasn't brand new, but it was a lovely shade of rose-red and knew it showed off every curve of her body. She did water wheels in the warm water, swam several long strokes back and forth, and enjoyed the sun. Ned swam along next to her and back, never far away. Noonan and Travis watched from the boat, in a private conversation.

At last, Noonan made a hard turn east and back to the boatyard.

The awkward moment finally came upon them as Noonan slowed the Bones and turned over the bumpers while Travis and Ned allowed the graceful insertion, tying her off.

Noonan placed Madison's camera in his duffel added the object, which was staining everything red and muddy despite being wrapped in a towel. He wiped down the bridge and then connected the electronics from the pier.

Ned walked alongside her as she held her wet suit over one arm, swinging her pink flippers back and forth as they traversed the gardens of the club in silence. Noonan had told them not to expect to go out tomorrow, so that left the calendar wide open. She had three glorious days off where no one expected her. Ned was here on vacation, at Noonan's beck and call. It was all lining up to be something more than a treasure dive.

At the edge of the parking lot, Ned placed his palm at the side of her face.

"I had a good time. I'd like to take this a little farther if you're willing, Madison."

That was a good line. Not cheesy. Not practiced. Could Ned be one of the last really good guys? Could she ever live with herself if she didn't give whatever it was he was offering a try?

The answer to that was no.

She dropped her fins and pack the same time his other hand came up to her face. She held her breath while he slowly arched down, touched her lips gently with his and then pulled back. She didn't discourage him, instead wrapping one arm around his waist and letting her fingers search up his back to pull him down to her. He exhaled and pressed against her mouth in a deep, exploratory kiss.

She was glad she'd taken hold of his waist or else she would have been washed out to sea.

CHAPTER 13

IT HAD BEEN years since Ned had felt the kind of urgency he had this afternoon. It just wasn't his style. He was good at going slow, taking his time, showing respect for the lady if he had designs on her. But the truth was, he'd never met that many women he urgently wanted to be with. Not like Madison. Not the way he felt today. Something pulled at him in ways he'd never felt before. Sex was never just sex for Ned, and that's why it hadn't come up that often during his first years in the Navy, even when everyone else was going out getting laid just to be doing it. Intimacy was about sharing something special with someone else, not blindly slapping thighs and getting it on like an animal.

But today, he wanted all of it—the sex, the talking with his fingers, exploring with his body in non-verbal ways he'd never done before.

The attraction he felt for Madison came clear out of

the blue, taking over. He watched her drive, watched as the wind blew her blonde hair off her face. He couldn't focus on anything else.

He toyed with her hair, interfering with her driving and making her laugh. With that bit of encouragement, he separated her long braids and combed her long locks with his fingers. He slid as close to her as he could, then kissed her ear, pressing her hair behind, then delicately kissed her neck. Her soft moan urged him on. He felt her pulse quicken where he kissed her. She gripped the steering wheel tightly.

By the time they arrived at her cottage, her shorts were unzipped and hanging off one hip. His pants were sliding so much he was practically bunny hopping the few steps to her front door. He kicked off his canvas slip-ons and tore off his shirt, watching her slide those shorts down slowly in a tease. She slipped her shirt over her head and walked slowly, one foot in front of the other, to where he was pinned on the couch, desperately trying to get his khakis off without showing her his red, white and blue shorts.

She kneeled over him, her breasts ripe and tasting sweet, all puckered and full as he played with her. His hands gripped her ass and squeezed, causing her to moan and lean into him as he buried his face in her chest.

"Do we have anything?" he asked. "I didn't—"

She slowly shook her head. "Sorry, but I'm on the pill."

"Should we wait?"

She slowly shook her head again.

His fingers slipped under her lap, rimming her opening. She raised one hip, stared at him with her azure blue eyes, balanced herself on his tip, and then pulled herself down on him.

The feeling of joining with her was exquisite. With her hands braced on his shoulders, she bounced up and down on him, sometimes looking down and touching his shaft where he entered her. Her breathing grew heavy as he stretched and slid along the sides of her sex, pushing in places, rubbing in others. Between each thrust, they watched each other, registering how right and beautiful it felt, their bodies mated as one.

He adjusted his hips to soar up and into her, sending her higher on his lap, deepening his penetration of her channel, driving her into little ripples of pleasure. She answered his thrusts by squeezing her internal muscles, and each time, he grew bigger, wanted her harder and faster.

She clutched her breasts, arched back, and begged for him to take her again. She lifted her right knee, and he helped her rise up, only for her to come crashing down on him. Up and down she used her leg to give traction, riding him, sheathing him in her warm juices, all the while asking for more. Her pink lips sucked his. Her little mewling sounds whispered into his ear nearly drove him over the edge. His hands explored the soft moistness beneath her breasts, squeezing her nipples and then hungrily plunged his tongue into her mouth.

He felt her heart beating frantically as their undulations continued, and then she started to shatter. He removed his hands from her backside and held her face watching the ecstasy fall like a wave across her cheeks and lips. Her eyes fluttered. She inhaled, her body burning with her desire. He stilled so she could feel the full force and power of her beautiful orgasm and kissed her neck until her breathing slowed and she opened her eyes.

Those blue eyes hooked everything he had inside. He was far from done with her. The edges of her lips curled. Her pink lips pouted again as she kissed him.

"Nice," he whispered. "This is so nice. I could do this all night."

Her smile got crooked as she continued her undulations. Her fingers ringed his shaft and they both looked down at their joining. She leaned into him, and then leaned back as he held on, squeezing her buttocks.

He was frustrated he couldn't get deep enough. She rode his groin as he thrust, pumping furiously, then holding her hips tight against him as he rammed himself deep with quick motions.

Her arms wrapped around his neck, her legs wide at the sides, so he picked her up and carried her into the bedroom, still fully seated inside her.

Her bed was covered with pillows like a field of flowers. With one sweep of his arm he sent the pillows flying except one pink heart. He lay her down tenderly and tucked it under that beautiful ass of hers, propping her pelvis up until fully available to him. The pink lips of her sex opened before him like petals as he played with her bud and got her writhing on the bed. He bit the inside of her thigh, traced her opening with his thumb, and then pressed her nub before slipping two fingers inside her. She moaned, arching backward. He moved her knee over in front of her, spread her cheeks and entered her from the side, holding her belly with his palm and pressing her against him. He thrust deep, pressing hard.

Her breathing became ragged. Her hands flew up, covering her face as her sweet lips called to him.

"Yes. Oh please."

He felt her loss of control as she began to shudder. He quickened his movements, expanding the crescendo overtaking her body. He added to the fire of her climax by pulling out and lapping her juices. Her fingers gripped his shoulders as he drank from her, flicked her bud with his tongue back and forth, and lazily inserted two fingers. She went wild, gripping the sheets at her sides and rocking up and down into his face.

He was getting close to orgasm himself. She spread her lips, massaging her own nub, then brought his face down on her, before drawing him up to her and locking him in a deep kiss. She angled her pelvis until his shaft was snagged on her opening again, and with one more thrust, he was inside again furiously pumping.

He was getting harder, his girth expanding. He moved back and forth against her as she moaned, shook and squeezed him inside.

He flipped her over and entered her from behind, hoisting her hips up into him as he pressed, pushing all the way to his hilt and holding her there until he could feel her insides fluttering again, milking his shaft.

He slid the pillow under her belly, kissed her shoulder, and fondled her bud with his right hand until she started to moan again. His hip movements were fast, getting faster.

"Is this how you like it, Maddie?" he whispered in her ear.

"God yes! Don't stop." She reached back and squeezed his left butt cheek.

"I have no intention of stopping."

He altered the pace, slowing, kneeling back and letting her change positions again so that they were facing one another. His fingers lazily snaked through her scalp as he explored the beauty of her face. He placed her legs up over his shoulders and began the long rhythmic way home, the slow penetrations gradually getting faster and faster until at last he felt her muscles clamp down on him and he reflexively burst inside her, plunging and spilling, filling her with everything he had as her head tossed from side to side. She gasped, pressing his buttocks against her and then held him there.

Her arms flapped to the sides like a rag doll. Ned covered them with his own, clutching her fingers between his and resting his head against her chest as he caught his breath. Her soft body, tanned and lithe, drew out of him all the monsters of loneliness and his thirst for relevance.

He knew he wasn't done fucking her. It would be food for his soul, watching her come, seeing the way her breasts shook in the late afternoon sun, exploring all the places where the delicate fine hairs on her body lay like gold against her flesh. He craved to bring her to the edge again and again, and then set her free, feeling the power of his desire for this beautiful woman who had opened up all the parts of himself he'd closed down years ago.

There wasn't any logic to it. He had a need of her that would never be satisfied.

Finally, the sunset was upon them, sending orange fire onto the walls of the bedroom as they watched it set in each other's eyes. He had never found such peace in a woman's arms before. She was quite simply, perfect in every way he could imagine, the answer to all the questions he'd had about the world. He was all in and completely captured.

"Do you like to swim naked in the ocean, Ned?" she whispered.

"Don't think I've ever done it," he answered, tracing her lower lip with his forefinger.

"Would you like to try it? With me?"

"I'll do anything with you, Madison."

"Anything? Isn't that dangerous?"

"No. It used to be, but not any longer. This is right, Madison. You feel it, too, I know."

"I do."

"So if you want to swim in the gulf naked, I'll be right there beside you."

She got up slowly, combing her hair with her fingers. Her long torso, her nude sex, and her perfect-shaped breasts with her pert upturned nipples were a wonder. He held her hand and allowed her to pull him off the bed.

"Hop on," he said, bending over. She climbed his back, holding onto his shoulders and wrapping her legs around his waist. "Blanket, please," he whispered, taking her over to the bed and lowering one knee, so she could pull one of the sheets. "I'm not wanting to get arrested and have to spend a night in jail," he laughed.

"Only if I could be there with you."

With the sheet around her shoulders, he ran through the back door, over the sand dunes and onto the beach. He knew his ass was in full view of the sunset watchers as he ran, the sheet streaming behind them like a cape. She was giggling, laughing and celebrating his run until they hit the water. He let her slide down, picked up the sheet and tossed it onto the sand. Her naked body frolicked in the surf until he caught her and pulled her down and they tumbled in the tiny waves, rolling over and over on the wet sand. He picked her up and threw her over the next wave, then dove in beneath her and brought her up to the top again. He rolled over on his back and kicked, while she worked to keep up with him until they got out to the deeper water.

He held her with one arm around her waist while they both tread water, facing the sunset.

She watched the dying sun, and he watched it in her eyes and face. He'd never been happier. She threw her arms around his shoulders again, pulling her knees up and wrapping them around his torso. Leaning back, he floated with her body on top. One hand stroked her backside from her neck to the top of her thigh.

"Are you sure you weren't born in the ocean? Maybe you're descended from a God."

He liked that thought. "And you are my mermaid, my muse."

"What have we started, Ned?"

"Something better than treasure. Whatever it is, I never want it to end."

"Me neither. Me neither."

It wasn't the water but tears she shed as he kissed her again.

"I like it deep and dangerous," she whispered into his ear.

He felt the space between her thighs, running along the lips of her sex with his forefinger but not penetrating. "Right up to the edge, Maddie, and then I'll save you. I'll get you in the middle of danger. Then I'll go in deep and save you every time."

She clung to him as he paddled back toward the shore and quickly retrieved the sheet to protect their nakedness. Together, they walked back to the cottage. He heard a couple of people clapping. Someone else shouted something he couldn't quite hear.

He looked down at her. "Did we make a stir?"

"I think so," she whispered back. "But I think they liked it."

As they got to the back door, he picked her up and

carried her into the bathroom. "Time for a hot shower and shampoo. All I can say, Maddie, is your neighbors better get ready, because I'm just getting started."

CHAPTER 14

T HEY STAYED IN bed the entire next day. Only thing that was part of her normal routine was the coffee in the morning, which she brought to him. He barely let her drink hers.

They ate fruit when they were hungry, sipped some white wine she had opened in the refrigerator, and munched on some cheese and almonds, but mostly the day was about sex. The natural way their bodies worked together was thrilling.

Ned kissed her. "That's what I love about you. It's fresh, honest. You don't hide anything."

"Well, I wouldn't go that far!"

"I know it's true because I'm the same way. I've never met anyone like you, Madison. Never."

"Kiss me, Ned."

He kissed her lips, her eyelids, her neck under both ears, the palms of her hands, and then back to her lips.

"I want us to stay like this, always," he whispered as

his hand smoothed over her hip and thigh, back and forth. He dipped his head and kissed her breast. "Connected, feasting on each other," he said as he angled his head, pulling her hair back behind her ear. "Touching the treasure of your golden body."

His tenderness moved her. She let the backs of her fingers sweep across his cheek. She'd always fallen for the bad boys. The strays in life. What was that all about? Always trying to heal someone broken. There wasn't a single thing about Ned that was broken.

She'd been thinking about her conversation with her mother and decided to bring it up.

"I figured out something, Ned."

"What?"

She propped herself up on her elbow, the sheet wrapped around her body. Ned pulled it back with his forefinger because it was blocking his view.

"Go on," he said after he kissed and nuzzled her nipples thoroughly.

"I think my mother was in love with your father."

He stopped.

"Your father is the *someone special* who perhaps broke her heart."

"You think so?" He was still kissing her chest.

"The pieces all fit. He comes out here to do a salvage with Noonan and meets her. They fall in love, but then he tells her he's married. He went back to California to be with your mother. Did you know that?"

Ned sat up, frowning. "He cheated on my mother?"

"I'm thinking so. My mother said this special person was a friend of Noonan's, and he went back to California to be with his wife. She told me he honored her by keeping his promise to his wife."

"Meaning if he'd have met your mother first and not second, you'd have been my sister, not my lover?"

She hit him with a pillow. "That's not funny."

"I think it's hilarious. Now the old bastard is somehow responsible for me finding you too. I can't get away from this jerk."

She hugged his back. "Ned, consider that he was a different person then. Don't you remember anything good about him? Anything at all?"

"He kept to himself. My biggest problem was that he wasn't very affectionate to my mom. I don't remember when that happened. But she loved something about him."

"Everyone deserves that," she said, rubbing his upper arm with her hand, back and forth. "Consider what my mother told me. He honored *her* with the right decision. He did the right thing. He was married. He never came back."

"But why, Madison? If he loved her?"

"Because he could put it aside to do the right thing. Maybe he did it for you. Have you ever thought about that?"

She considered perhaps she'd burdened him with too much talk about the past. Maybe Ned's father always expected to come right back into her mother's house one day if and when his wife was taken first. But it happened the other way around. Fate made him an honorable man.

At the cost of his soul.

It was just a theory, though. Madison had never met the man nor Ned's mother. But there was something in Ned's DNA that brought him back to Florida, and yes, perhaps his father had paved the way.

"Have I upset you?" she asked, rubbing the tops of his shoulders and squeezing the nape of his neck.

"I don't want to be mothered. I don't want your help, if that's what you're asking."

She was surprised at his tone.

"Explain."

He turned on the bed, crossed his legs, and faced her. "Madison, this is my life. This is your life. It has nothing to do with the past. This is about the here and now, about us, and what we make of it. I don't need to think about the past. I don't need to know or even suppose all this is connected like some cosmic mystery. My mind doesn't work that way. I don't worry about the choices I made or what my dad did. It has nothing to do with me. That was his life."

He couldn't see the blind spot that was the size of the Titanic, the flaw in his thinking. But she saw it, and to herself she heard the truth.

Everything is always connected. It's one big circle.

There was the cook who took his little dog, Otis, on a voyage. The cook's wife wore the necklace that was a gift of the governor's wife. The family of that woman wanted to find that necklace, lost at the bottom of the Gulf at Treasure Island, where her mother and his father were once lovers. It *was* all connected.

It would be hard to prove this to him, and perhaps he didn't need that. But just like love, she couldn't prove it existed, but she knew it was real.

CHAPTER 15

NOONAN CALLED A meeting of the crew. Madison took Ned back to his place so he could put on some fresh clothes.

"Just move out," she said. "Stay with me. It's only for a few more days. Maybe you'd decide to stay here."

Looking up at her while he rummaged through his duffel, he was tempted to tell her what she obviously wanted to hear. Heck, he wanted to say it, too. But something was clouding the back of his mind, and until he figured it out, he wasn't going to commit.

There's that logic creeping back in.

It was almost like he was two separate men. One made careful, slow decisions, and now he had spawned this other Ned—the impulsive one who would throw away anything to be with her. And he barely knew her.

His logic side won out, convinced that if they were meant to be, she'd be patient to wait just a little bit longer until he could settle what was going on inside him.

He held his arms out to the sides, still seated on the bed. "Come here, Madison."

She sat in his lap, her legs stretching over his thighs with her right arm wrapped around his shoulder.

"Time for a little talk."

He could feel her tense.

"No, not *that* kind of a talk. There's no question you and I have made this connection and that we were destined to find each other. It makes no sense at all, but it's true. But it's like we're setting out on this journey in a dinghy. We're talking about the ocean here. Unless you were talking about some beach or vacation romance, and for the record," he leaned over and planted a soft kiss on her lips, "I'm not."

She sighed, pressing the side of her face against his. "I ache so bad for you, Ned. Don't scare me like that."

"Hey!" He turned her head by tipping her chin. "I need this. I want this, Madison. I've just arrived here, and my whole life has changed. I can forget about it when we're in bed together. I want it to last forever. But I can't wish away what my past is. What my job is. And you wouldn't want me to anyway."

It broke his heart that he could feel hers pumping so fiercely, and not because of her feelings for him, but because she was afraid. He realized he was too. And there it was again, that past. Just like his father, he was caught in two worlds, two realities. Ned didn't want to make the choice his father did, not only because it was his father's way, but because he wanted to have it all. And that's what he hadn't figured out yet.

She began to stand, and he knew she was frustrated again. He grabbed her arm and brought her back to his lap. "Trust me, Madison. I'm slow. I don't do things like this. God help me, but I think about things maybe too much, but it's also who I am and how I've been trained. But I always figure it out eventually. What I want to give you is more than a couple of fun days in bed and some sexy time at the beach. I want to give you so much more."

She hugged him, kissed his ear, and whispered, "Don't take too long, Ned. Don't break my heart."

"Never," he whispered back as he held her tight. "If I come walking through your door with all my stuff, I'm never leaving."

Her blue eyes teared up.

"I'm like that guy in the movie who found a mermaid and tried to take her home. In the end, he had to let her go to save her life."

"Her name was Madison."

"Really? I didn't know that. You are my mermaid. But ours is a different story."

Their kiss was deep. The feel of her tears brushing against his cheek, he took as her honest gift. She trusted that he wouldn't break her heart, and he'd keep that promise. But he didn't want to live one life and wish he'd lived another. He couldn't do that to her.

"I have something for you," he said as he stood, holding her with his arm around her waist. "Close your eyes." His impulsive side had completely taken over, and Ned let him rip.

She did as was told. Digging around in his bag, he found the book of poetry, which he'd go over with her later, then found the velvet bag with the pendant in it. He unclasped it and placed it around her neck. He was fully aware of the valuable gift he was bestowing on a near-stranger. Except she wasn't really a stranger. And maybe the mermaid his father had fallen in love with was gone, but Ned's mermaid was here, in front of him.

She held her fingers to the pendant and opened her eyes without being told. Turning to see herself in the dresser mirror, he placed his hands on her shoulders. With his face next to hers, he whispered, "He found this here. I'm returning it to where it belongs. I think it was really meant for you."

Her shocked expression and the floodgate of tears warmed him.

"I can hardly see it through my tears, Ned. Oh, it's priceless!"

"He was with Noonan when they found this. He

used to wear it all the time, and I resented him for not giving it to my mother."

He turned her to face him, cupping her face between his hands. "He used to say all the time that he'd had a secret love with a mermaid. I think he intended that I give it to mine."

"But your mother—"

"Never claimed ownership. She wouldn't have worn it, ever. My mother had all the rest of him."

She turned back to look at herself again. "It's the most precious thing I've ever owned, Ned. But with all your family history, are you sure? I don't want to take a family heirloom."

He chuckled. "Oh, but I've been thinking about what you'd look like with it on for the past day. It's just a pendant. I already gave you my heart."

Noonan's phone call interrupted their kisses.

"Yes, Boss?"

"Where the hell are you guys? I've been waiting here for a half hour, dammit. We have things we need to go over, and right away."

"Got it. We'll be right there."

"I'm assuming you're with Madison 'cause she didn't pick up, either."

"You'd be right," he said, smiling at her fingers covering her lips.

"Well, dammit, get your clothes on and get down

right away."

"You got it."

He shrugged. Her eyes were still sparkling, remnants of her tears collecting in the sides of her eyes.

"Duty calls." He pulled her against him. "But I can't wait to fulfill all those dreams I had about you wearing only this as I watched you call my name." He brushed the hair back from her face, kissed her forehead, and did a quick change while she looked on.

On their way out, Ned noticed a skinny dog sleeping on the deck outside the back door. If he'd had more time, he'd have fed the poor animal. But before he could make it out of the doorway, he reconsidered.

"Just a sec. I saw something I just have to take care of."

"What?" she asked.

Ned pulled down a can of beef stew he'd bought, emptied it into a dish, then filled a small plastic bowl with water, and gave it to Madison.

At the door, the dog lifted up his head and began to skitter off toward the beach.

"Here you go, boy. I've got some food for you," he said, extending the bowl toward the scrawny animal. He laid it down and took Madison's bowl, setting the water beside it before backing away. He stepped inside the living room, closing the door.

The two of them watched as the dog sniffed the

food and then started gulping it down. Ned could see the ribs on the side of the mutt and wondered if a previous owner living here had left him behind. He was heartened that the dog ate.

"Aww. Poor thing. I'm so glad you fed him. I can't imagine how some people treat their pets," she said.

"I'll get some regular food maybe tonight. See if he comes back. But that should do him some good now."

Ned was happy he'd solved his conscience. The brownish mutt looked up at him with warm brown eyes and licked his nose. The bowl was empty.

It made him proud to be that kind of a man.

"JESUS FUCKIN' CHRIST," Noonan said, checking his watch. "Don't they teach you to be on time? You start all your missions like forty minutes late?" he barked at Ned.

They had agreed to meet at Flamingo Pete's, a crusty bar up the road in Indian Shores. Ned understood Noonan was trying to be stealth about his new find.

Travis had a stupid expression on his face and had devoured a plate of French fries. Noonan didn't even ask if anyone wanted to eat.

"What did you find out?" Ned asked, not addressing Noonan's dig.

They were seated at a high table off in the corner

near the parking lot. Traffic noise made listening difficult, but Ned knew it was chosen for that reason.

"I got a friend who does these subcontracts out to bigger dive companies. They hire him when they get a good lead. Otherwise, he goes out on his own. He said there was a buzz about ten years ago about something, but he looked into it and can't find a claim. I don't want to show my face around the office. I tried Googling the area and can't find a damned thing. But ten years ago? I mean there wasn't that much out there. At least not on this coast.

"He checked archeological sites, not just pleasure dives?"

"He did. Looked up all the bigs and couldn't find anything. He was going to go back to the office on Monday to do some additional digging around, but we have a couple of choices."

They waited.

"We can file a claim, like the family did for the salvage. I mean, we have a right to be there. But we're supposed to let the State of Florida know what we suspect we've found. On the other hand, we could also tell the estate what we found on their dime, so to speak. I mean, it's a grey area."

"Who are they?" Madison asked.

"From North Carolina. Some businessman there owns furniture stores or something. I dealt with their attorney."

"So you're diving for people you don't really know?" asked Ned.

"Hey! May I remind you that you're in the same boat!"

"But I assumed—" Ned began to protest.

"You know what they say about that word. Look, we have to make a decision."

"What if we go back down there this weekend, look around, and then wait until your friend gets more information on Monday?" suggested Madison.

"We could. I mean, we are legally allowed to be there," Noonan answered.

"Let me get this straight. What you're saying is that there's the proper way, and then there's a smart way," added Ned.

"Yes. And either way could be dangerous. Not for finding a fuckin' dog collar. That was a no-brainer. No problem. But now, if we've found something big, well, people have disappeared over that. And if we report it to the State, there's no guarantee that someone doesn't get tipped off, you know. I mean, I want to trust everyone in government, but Ned, do I have to tell you there are dirty players out there, especially if we're talking about—"

Their waitress appeared, asking for their drink order. Before Ned could decline, Travis ordered a beer.

Ned knew Noonan wasn't happy with that. When the waitress went away, he scolded the young diver.

"Shit, Travis. We're trying to be left alone. Just where is your head at?"

Ned's growing concern over Travis as a dive partner was tarnished further. They all searched around them for signs anyone was interested in the foursome, waiting until the beer arrived, and then Ned continued.

"I like Madison's idea. We go look for something concrete first, something we can have verified before we make a claim."

Travis asked, "And what about the red rocks, Noonan? Anything come of them?"

"Mush. It might have been an iron tool of some kind. But it was like red pudding, just fell apart in my hands," said Noonan.

"That's too bad," whispered Madison. "I was hoping for something there."

Ned continued with his question. "What *are* the rules about this sort of thing? I mean, does the fact that you got the permission for the one dive mean that anything as a result of that dive is also theirs?"

"It could. One could argue either way. We were given the authority to keep some artifacts for ourselves, limited to a value of five hundred dollars. So we find a chest, something special, well, you couldn't argue that it was worth less than five hundred, could you?"

Travis suddenly pushed his arm across the table at Madison.

"Where'd you get that?" he said as he pulled the mermaid pendant with the eight coin up from her chest.

Noonan slapped his hand. "You don't touch a lady like that, you dumbass. That's her person and her stuff." He sat back and winked at Ned. There was a reason he didn't want to acknowledge the pendant to Travis, so Ned played along.

Madison was just as smart. "A friend of my mother's gave it to me." She tucked it into her shirt and added, "It's a replica. If it were the real thing, well, would I be wearing it around?"

Travis grinned, "Still a pretty nice piece. It suits you, Madison. I like it."

Ned's concern over their situation grew. He locked eyes with Noonan. He wished the old pirate hadn't included Travis in his findings. Maybe it would be a good idea to surgically remove him from the group, make up something to send him away thinking their find was not really the valuable wreck of a Spanish Galleon. It was all getting sticky.

But Noonan was being honorable to the young diver. "So I agree. We go down one more time, see if we can find anything we can research. And then we'll reassess on Monday after I hear from my buddy."

"I'm cool with that," said Travis.

Madison nodded. She looked at Ned. "Are we in?"

"Hell yeah," Ned answered.

"Okay, it's oh-eight-hundred, same place?" Noonan asked the group, and everyone agreed.

NED AND MADISON stopped at a local pet store and bought a small bag of kibble and some canned food to moisten it up.

"You mind slumming at my place tonight?" he asked her on the way back to his cottage.

"As long as I'm slumming with you, I don't. It does smell a little bit. Do you have any candles?"

"We'll get some."

They stopped at a beach shop where he let Madison pick out three pillars. He also bought some shampoo and shower gel and sweet-smelling hand soap. He knew ladies liked that sort of thing. This pad had never been intended to be a place to entertain her in.

They also bought some ice cream and stopped and ordered Mexican food to go.

The dog wasn't there when they returned. He left the water, but started another dish with the new food he bought, substituting it for the dirty one, before going inside to have their dinner.

Madison set one of the candles on the table between them. She placed another one in the bathroom with the shower gel and soap, and she placed the third one by his bed on the tiny bedside table. He liked watching her work her magic, setting up a stage for the evening, not being shy about what she wanted to do.

They ate without speaking. He was hungrier than he'd thought.

She leaned back, sipping on her beer. "Are you nervous about this?"

"No, not at all. I've made love to a woman before," Ned said with a completely straight face.

She rapid-blinked at the joke. "You know what I mean."

He pulled her hand to him and kissed her palm. "I do. I get your meaning. I'm on your wavelength. Totally." He followed it up with a smile as she put her hand back in her lap.

He picked up the two empty containers, taking them to the trash in the kitchen. "Ice cream?"

"Maybe later?"

"I think you're gonna be busy later. No time for ice cream."

"Depends on how you use it."

He'd opened the gallon lid and was just about to scoop himself a large bite. He stopped mid-air and pointed the spoon at her. "You have a point there. I might need further instruction. Should I bring it into the bedroom then?" He raised his eyebrows like he was waiting for her command.

"No. I have something else in mind, first."

"Okay. She's being all mysterious tonight." He put the lid back on the ice cream and placed the spoon in the sink.

"I'm not being mysterious at all. I just find there are things more important than ice cream. First things first. And then dessert. That's just the way I look at it."

He quickly arrived at her side, pulled her up, and started to remove her blouse.

Behind him, he heard a bark. The dog had finished the plate of food Ned brought him and walked away.

"He says he likes it," said Madison.

"Oh, so mermaids talk to dogs, do they?" he said while he removed her bra and gasped at the look of her breasts with the pendant hanging between them.

"They do."

"What else do they do?

"They have very sensitive fingers," she said as she slipped her hand inside his waistband and grabbed him.

"Oh, sweetheart, you are so right."

"They like deep diving too."

"I can just bet they do." He knelt before her, unzipped her jeans, and pulled her pants down to her knees. He placed his hand on the juncture between her thighs. He rubbed her panties back and forth, curling two fingers to fondle the ridge between her lips. "They love to dive for buried treasure," he said as he exhaled and slipped her panties down over her jeans.

As his fingers breached her swollen lips, he felt her hands on his shoulders. She leaned over, spread her knees, and gave him access. His tongue slid inside her opening. He leaned back and looked up at her.

"Nice. You are so sweet." With one arm under her knees and the other under the small of her back, he picked her up, her jeans still flapping behind. Until he could remove everything.

While he undressed, he watched her position herself back on his bed, prop her little butt under one of his pillows, and fondle the necklace glistening between her nipples.

She squeezed her little rosy pink areolas until they got stiff. She licked her lips. His cock was rock hard and ready. He wasn't going to think about anything else tonight except how many times he could make her come.

There would be time tomorrow for his logical side. But in the meantime, there was a lot of her golden flesh to kiss, to explore.

And there was a whole gallon of ice cream to eat.

CHAPTER 16

TRAVIS AND NOONAN were waiting for them when she and Ned arrived. They were a whole ten minutes early. They'd even had time to take a morning run on the beach. Their stray followed them part of the way then greeted them when they returned. He was left with some food. Neither one of them were able to touch him yet.

Madison's wetsuit and flippers were loaded. Ned grabbed his equipment from the pile Noonan had once again assembled on the pier and checked it.

The morning was a little cooler with fingers of light grey fog stretching out into the gulf like those of a skeleton. No one was out yet, but Sundays were light days, especially for the drinking crowd, Noonan told them.

He let Travis pilot the boat for a bit while he grabbed the two of them, directing them down into the galley for coffee.

"What's up?" Ned asked as he was handed his coffee.

"My guy called me last night and asked if we'd said anything to anybody."

"Uh oh," said Madison. She knew there was the only one place such a leak would come from.

"I knew it, dammit." Ned started grinding his teeth.

"I'm gonna tell my friend to just file a damned claim for us tomorrow. Try to make a mistake on the coordinates and correct them later."

Madison didn't know that was an option. "Aren't you going to confront him?"

"Trouble with all these treasure seekers, they all try to stay secretive. Like pulling teeth to get anything out of my buddy. He just left it at that; it was a rumor."

"Could be the old rumor," Ned added.

"The coincidence is uncanny," Noonan said. "I don't trust him. But then, who would Travis know? He doesn't know anybody. He's not plugged in at all."

Madison disagreed. She knew if there was one rumor it had the potential to get out of control. "You have to find out who he talked to about our dive. Maybe someone knew he was going and got it out of him. Someone could have just been smarter."

"I'm with Madison. I think someone's just fishing."

"Well, I'm going to have a little talk with him when I go up top. Just keep your eyes and ears open. Let me know if you see anything about him that sets you funny," sighed Noonan.

"I wanna search his pack." Ned wasn't kidding.

Madison thought it was an excellent idea.

"Go ahead, but I don't want to know about it, okay?"

"Agreed. Unless I find something."

"I'm going up. Make it quick. I'll make sure he's tied up for ten or so."

After Noonan climbed the ladder, Ned grabbed the diver's backpack and unzipped the large side first. He found a hash pipe and a small tin foil wad in a baggie.

"Fuckin' drugs," he muttered.

"That's not bad, Ned. You should see what people do here," she added.

Ned continued with his search and found a cell phone, a change of shorts, some candy, a soda can, and a small wad of dollars.

"Doesn't look like anything here is out of the ordinary."

Madison unzipped the small bottom pocket and found a sketchbook and black felt tipped pen. She flipped through the pages. Travis was actually a fairly good artist, which surprised her. The last page drawn on was a sketch of the anchor. She held it up to Ned.

"Sonofabitch."

"Might not mean anything. He might not have

shown it to anyone," she said.

"It depends where he drew it. I don't like it."

"He doesn't say where it came from. It could have been an illustration from a book, for all anyone knows."

"Why are you defending him?"

"I'm not. I'm just thinking you're getting a little paranoid, that's all."

"You haven't seen the kinds of things out there I have. There are people who will sell their children to get their hands on something that has the potential to make them some money. The world is a very wicked place."

"I know, but don't make things up that don't exist, Ned. This isn't proof he showed anybody."

"But—"

Noonan's booming voice told them to get topside.

A rubber pontoon boat with several divers lay off to their left. The fog had partially obscured them. Madison wondered if they'd followed the group.

"Who are they?" asked Ned.

"I think they're just weekend divers," said Travis.

"How do you know that?" Noonan drilled him. "You know any of the guys over there?"

"I can't tell. But no, I don't think so. I don't know anyone that has an inflatable like that. They're all in black. Look like research grunts to me," answered

Travis.

"We're changing course," Noonan said and took over the wheel. He passed a map to Travis. "Find me something over here," he said pointing to a deep portion of the gulf. "I'm going to pretend we're on our way over there. I don't want them following us."

Travis pointed out the notation of a fishing vessel that sank ten years previous. "We could be doing a recovery dive there."

As Noonan veered left, the boat next to them continued straight ahead, right toward the spot they intended to explore, disappearing into the mist.

"Shit," he muttered under his breath.

But they stuck to their plan, even went so far as to prepare for a dive. Noonan shut the motor down and was preparing to drop the anchor. Travis slipped off his khakis and tee shirt then put the wetsuit on over his underwear. He folded his clothes, leaving them in a plastic cubby, placing his red cell phone on top.

Madison noted that the other phone Ned found in the galley was brown. She held the phone up so Ned would see it. Noonan was perplexed.

Ned picked Travis up under his arms and threw him overboard before he had any of his gear on. The metal detector crashed in behind him.

Travis scrambled to retrieve it. "Hey! What the hell was that for? You asshole. Keep your hands off me."

"Who'd you tell, Travis?" asked Ned, leaning over the boat.

"What do you mean? Tell what?"

"Crank her over, Noonan. Let's see how bad he wants to talk."

Before Noonan could turn the key, Travis was sputtering, screaming, "No!" He swam to climb up the ladder, the metal detector in his left hand. Ned grabbed the machine and then kicked Travis in the chest, sending him backward into the water again.

"Who was it? You're not getting back on this boat until you tell me."

"How the fuck? Oh, come on, Noonan. This guy's wacko."

"Tell him what he wants to know," shouted Noonan.

Travis hit the water with his fist, "Fuck!"

Madison could see no one was going to budge. Noonan edged closer to Ned. "You wanna explain this to me?"

"He's got two cell phones. Either one of them could track us. He has a sketch in his backpack of the anchor."

"All right. Let me explain. Can I come up now?" Travis pleaded.

Noonan helped him up the ladder and threw a towel at him. Ned ran below decks and came up with the other phone, which he held in front of Travis' face.

"They told me to call them when we got to the site. Look, you're gonna file a claim anyway, and you have the right to be there, like you said."

"Who are they, Travis?" asked Noonan.

"They're just kids. Went to high school with them. Look, they don't dive. They don't know what the fuck they're doing."

"So why do they care about the coordinates?" Ned asked.

"I don't know. They just gave me a hundred bucks to do it. That's all. Honest, I didn't tell them anything."

"How did they know then?" he asked again.

"I scored some weed from one of them. I owe him a little bit for it, and I told him I was going to be paid for this dive, and he agreed to wait. When I got back, he was waiting for me, and I told him we were going back, but I didn't have anything for him yet. But I promised I would. When he asked about it, I told him I couldn't talk about it."

Both Ned and Noonan swore at the same time.

"You are a fuckin' idiot, Travis," barked Noonan.

"They aren't connected to any of this stuff. I don't even know if they swim. I do a little bit of drugs with them, nothing bad, a little stuff here and there to take the edge off."

"You don't have anything you need to take the edge

off except the occasional thought running through that pea-sized brain about getting a job. You just have to get high until that little 'feeling' goes away. You're off this dive, Travis," yelled Noonan.

Madison didn't know what they would do. If they went back to the dock, tossed Travis, and then went back out, it might attract too much attention.

"We can't risk it. We have to go back." Noonan looked like he could throw everyone overboard; he was so angry.

"I say we go out, but he stays in the boat. Maddie and I can take the gear," said Ned.

"You could come with us, Noonan," Maddie suggested. "Travis can watch the bridge."

"Nope. Not putting my boat in the hands of a kid who did this."

Madison knew he was thinking about it, seriously. Finally, he made a decision.

"Okay, you two go. Travis and I stay up top," Noonan finally mumbled.

"Then let's crank her up. First, we get rid of this." Ned pitched the brown phone as far as he could, where it made a tiny splash and disappeared.

Noonan grabbed Travis' other phone and pitched it as well.

"Hey!" Travis protested.

"So you get a new phone out of me. You get to be

the dumbass, and I have to buy you a new fuckin' phone. But I don't trust you with either. Ned, Madison, I want your phones."

"Hold up, I'm not throwing my phone overboard," objected Ned.

"No, I just want to hold on to them to make sure he doesn't give out a signal. That's all."

Travis sulked with his arms crossed over his chest. Noonan started the motor, and Madison watched Ned slip on his wetsuit, sliding the zipper up his front slowly, giving her a wink. He helped her zip up hers and then planted a kiss on her lips.

"Here's to another adventure."

She'd been sure she didn't want to fall for danger-ous guys, but what they were going to do was dangerous. She sat next to Ned as the boat turned, heading North East, holding his hand and enjoying the feel of his warmth as their thighs touched.

CHAPTER 17

IF THIS HAD been a mission for work, he'd have a boatload of guys who could probably overtake an oil tanker, subdue the crew, and drive the thing back to port. They even used to joke about it. He had backup and backup for his backup. He'd be properly armed. They'd have some of the best equipment made and all the experience and training necessary to use it.

But this was different. He didn't even have his sidearm. He had his KA-BAR, but a lot of good that would do except punch a hole in that big grey bubble of a speedboat. Noonan's electronic equipment was easily twenty years old, and what had been upgraded had been a patch job. He had wires held together with duct tape. He had cracks in the hull of the boat repaired with some kind of super glue. One of the outboards was smoking, and that worried him, too.

Noonan, while he might have been fit at one time, was not the man he was as a Navy diver. Like his dad, he'd aged. Ned had seen those pictures of the two of them standing together. They had both been rugged and built and could handle long swims, planting explosive devices and helping the Coasties before the drug problem got as bad as it did. They rescued distressed families that had been victimized by pirates and sailors unlucky to be abandoned at sea.

But Noonan wasn't in that shape any longer. He only had one eye, which meant, even if he had a weapon, he wouldn't be reliable. Their third was Travis, who had created the problem in the first place and whose loyalties were questionable.

And then of course there was Madison. She was the fittest person on the team besides him. She had the drive and the smarts. But she'd not been trained, and if anything happened to her, he would never be able to live with himself.

In addition, she was a beautiful woman, eye candy. He had no right getting her into this vulnerable spot.

It was a risk. If the bad guys were anywhere near where they were heading, he'd make sure they turned back and gave up on the search. So his logical side calculated that it was a risk, but perhaps one worth taking. As long as everything looked doable.

Noonan's boat would still outrun the other one. He was used to these waters and the weather was good, except for the mist that was now dissipating. Soon it would be hot. No bad weather in sight, and no clouds even.

He knew how people got hooked on treasure. He'd heard the stories. Like the gold fever was in California during the rush. Kings ransomed their kingdoms for a tulip bulb at one time. There was a chance that they could secure something that could set him up for life. Noonan deserved it too. Even Travis could come away with something. If they did this properly, they might be able to claim their treasure. There were a lot hurdles to climb, but he allowed himself to enjoy the fantasy.

He and Maddie could get a fine house by the beach and just sleep and make love for the first year then figure out the rest of their lives after that. That's what he was going for. That brass ring.

The necklace his dad brought back was proof that fortunes were made out here in the waters off the Florida coast. People had blind luck all the time and went home rich. What were the odds they could start out looking for a dog collar and find the motherlode? They all deserved that shot.

He used Noonan's binoculars to scan the horizon constantly as they traveled. He searched every inch of water, every ocean swell. Much easier to spot another boat when it was calm too. Lots of things made this find a possibility. It was as if the ocean was laying low for them, calling them to come take her, plunder her wealth and then spend the rest of his life worshiping her.

Noonan raised his eyebrows, and Ned shook his head.

Travis looked bored, leaning on one arm and then sulking and finally falling asleep.

Noonan checked with him one more time. Ned stood this time, scanned the whole gulf in a three-sixty as the boat slowed. Noonan was paying attention to his coordinates, watching the underwater topography dancing in green outline.

He joined Noonan at the bridge. "I don't see a thing. We have a perfect day for this too," he told his father's friend.

"Thanks, Son." He killed the motor and glanced over at Travis who threw over his light anchor while the winch released the other one, which hit bottom at seventy-five feet.

"You see anybody, you let us know. Don't try to be a hero," he cautioned Noonan. "Are you sure you're going to be okay?"

"I'm fine. I feel kind of bad about the kid," Noonan shrugged. Travis was still giving him death stares. "He's harmless. Stupid as hell," Noonan let his voice carry so Travis could hear it. "But he's just a dumb kid. I did stuff when I was young, too, that I now regret."

"Anything else we should look for?"

"Just get some good pictures. Don't spend too much time on the anchor and the cannon. Go farther in, maybe check on that debris wall. Oh, and I brought this." He pulled out a long canvas bag that looked like it held a pool cue. Inside was a wicked crowbar about two feet long, with a two-pronged edge on one end that could saw through wood, and a hook to use while climbing. The other end was fashioned in a smooth square tip, arched slightly like a regular crowbar, with a slot in the middle for removing nails or other pieces of metal.

"Where'd you get this?"

"One of my friends, God rest his soul, left it to me in his will."

"This thing looks like an ancient Viking grappling tool." Ned had never seen anything like it.

"Maybe it was fashioned after one. But it was made in the USA. Got that stamp right there."

Ned fingered over the flag and the words. "Son of a bitch."

They brought a plastic-coated wire basket that was sometimes used to catch lobster during their pleasure dives. Ned wound the crowbar through the mesh holes, securing two sides with plastic Velcro straps.

He adjusted his tool belt containing his KA-BAR and pulled on his one piece facemask. Madison was already at the back, sitting on the deck, dangling her flippers in the water. She was wearing the gloves Noonan provided them both, holding on to the metal detector.

"Can you hear me, sweetheart?"

"Yessir, I do."

"I'll follow you." He adjusted his feet into his own fins, slipped into his gloves, and shoved off the deck into the water.

Madison was first to check their coms under water. "I like that you and I can talk dirty now and no one will know."

"I never knew mermaids had such dirty minds."

"We've been holding out on all of you guys. We're more than a pretty face, you know."

"Tell me about it, Madison."

"Here, I turned it on for you." She handed him the metal detector. "Just pass it back if you want to trade off."

"Thank you, ma'am." The green screen was blank. He slipped the strap around his forearm, held it by the bicycle grip on the aluminum shaft, and angled the wire end in front of him as he followed her pink flippers down into the deeper water.

The turquoise water got darker, so he turned on his spotlight, which only made it worse, so he switched it off. Though the water was calm, a golden shower of sediment surrounded them, probably pieces of shells and rocks that picked up sunlight from above. A small school of yellow and black striped fish scurried around them, curiously interested in Madison's pink fins. She was descending slowly and then stopped to let the fish encircle her. "Look at these guys. My entourage!" she laughed.

"They love you, Madison. You're a mermaid. They like your fins and wish they had pink ones too."

She laughed as several of the larger ones allowed her to touch them carefully.

He followed her graceful legs deeper until they descended to the floor. They'd kicked up some silt, so waited for all the dust to settle before assessing their bearings.

The anchor and cannon were nowhere to be found. The debris field wasn't as richly laden with rocks and pieces of metal as before. He did a sweep with the detector, and it didn't register any metal. He thought perhaps there was a dark shadow several yards off to the right so he pointed.

"I'm looking for that wall of debris. I'm seeing a shadow over there. How about you?"

"Good eye. Put your light on."

He felt like an idiot forgetting the lamp. As soon as he switched it on, he found a row of timbers tied together with iron straps lying on the sand. Ends of the wood had been eaten away, and Madison could actually pull small chunks apart with her hands. Fragments of the old timbers dissolved into a cloud of silt, rising toward the surface.

He swung the detector over the platform, and it registered as he followed the bands of iron and the bolts, now concreted with ocean debris. He located a tiny hatch not more than two feet square. Inside, he flashed his light.

There were mounds of rocks scattered all over the floor inside the hatch.

"What do you see?" she asked him.

"Come take a look. Looks to me like remnants of soft cargo."

She floated near his face, and he illuminated the small hatch space. It was difficult to see anything that stood out to them as being metal until he saw what appeared to be a circular pile of red rocks.

"I'm going to guess a coil of chain, maybe?" she asked.

They followed along the top of the platform until it became buried in a debris field. More timbers laid across the space, and beyond, when he added light, he came to what looked like another wall of debris.

"This might be the backside of what we saw before. Doesn't look the same."

"No, it doesn't." She examined the pile of rotted timbers, covered in starfish and sea flowers. "Run the wand over here," she asked.

He traveled from the base of the wall up nearly fifteen feet. All along the way, the detector registered iron or nickel. Madison took pictures as they traveled the wall.

At the top, he crested what he was certain was remnants of a large wooden-hulled ship on its side. It appeared as if it had floated or been dragged over the timber platform, with pieces of lumber scattered all over where it inserted in the sand beyond, as if these pieces fell back onto the ship after the landing.

"Whoa!" Madison said. "I gotta get some pictures of this!"

They slowly examined the slightly curved structure, which was riddled with huge gaps where fish swam in and out. He noted part of a wooden railing. Madison documented the curve of an arched doorway.

There didn't appear to be anything left of the ship, really, except this piece. If there had been interior spaces, they were crushed during travel or when it landed. They cleared the hull remnants, coming to an eerily bare and pristine patch of white sand. Something lay on the floor, and at first glance, it appeared to be a body. He held up, showing Madison with his lamp.

"What is it?" she asked.

"You tell me. It can't be a body."

She was first to swim toward it. Then she stopped,

floating above it. "You won't believe this, Ned."

The net and metal detector were slowing him down, but as he approached and showed the light on the object, he stared back into the face of a woman. The statue of a female body was encrusted in sea scales and coral. Part of the colorful detail had been recently exposed, scraped off by some force of nature. Only the head and shoulders of the statue were visible. While Madison was photographing her, he removed a small shovel from his tool belt and tried to scrape the sand away. It hadn't been buried by centuries of debris. This was something that was recent or was recently unearthed.

He moved the metal detector over her body, and the machine lit up. Something was buried beneath her.

"Help me with this, Madison. Can you remove some of the sand holding her down?"

"This can't be wood, Ned. It looks like carved stone. Is it marble?"

He smoothed his fingers over her shoulder. Then he scraped it with the tip of his knife and then tapped it lightly.

"I think it is marble. It isn't painted, Madison. It's inlay."

It occurred to him that perhaps the object was newer than the age of a Spanish galleon.

They finished digging around the statue, revealing

her form had been broken just below her waist. The roughly four-foot section of her body was lifted carefully. They lay her back down on the white sand and set their attention to the dark stones beneath where she lay. It looked like she was lying in death over a pyre of coal.

The metal detector lit up and vibrated in his hand, registering eighty-eight.

Silver!

Rounded pieces, like charcoal, were scattered just as if someone built a fire beneath her. He was able to dislodge one of the pieces, handing it to Madison to document. She placed it in the basket. He removed several others, all of them slightly larger than a walnut. Madison took pictures of all of them and the area from which he'd pried them loose.

As he worked to dislodge another, a chunk with several clusters of what looked like black seeds the size of grapes came off. The detector also registered silver.

Madison looked up at him. "Do you want to go to another site to search?"

"I'm going to mark it, first." He tied a piece of red Velcro to a rod of crusted metal sticking out from the hull behind him.

"What about her?"

Ned considered whether it was wise to try to move her. If they dropped her, she might shatter as she fell back down into the wreck.

"Let's try it. Now I'm wishing we had Travis."

"I'll tell you right away," she said as she started to lift, "if I can't handle the weight."

He'd thought it would be lighter in water, but since it was a solid piece of stone, it wasn't. He tied the detector to his belt and tied his basket to Madison's, and they slowly ascended after pulling on the dive line three times and receiving the all clear in return.

As they neared the surface, Madison's grip was failing. Ned quickly untied the basket and let it float back down to the floor, encircling the lady of the sea's torso with the basket tie line. He knotted it and began to pull it toward the surface. He wasn't going to make it.

"Let's lash it to the dive line. Maybe if we get Noonan's help, we can get it up the rest of the way."

"Good idea." Madison swam around the body of the statue, entangling the dive line around her arms and her torso, being careful to avoid her neck area, which was the narrowest part.

Noonan must have sensed something was wrong and began pulling up as they pushed. Ned wished he could see the pirate's face when the body of a goddess popped up out of the water at him.

A net was thrown into the water, and he and Madison wrapped the lovely lady in it. They both watched as she was hauled up and out of the water with Noonan's winch.

"I'm going back to get the basket," he said.

"I'm coming with you."

"No—"

"Nonsense. It's the rules. Pairs. Never dive alone, Ned, you know that. Even for a quick dive to the bottom."

The dive line was thrown back into the water. He encircled Madison's waist as her arms held him around the shoulders and they pulled themselves down hand-over-hand using the line to descend.

"You are a mermaid. You belong under water, Madison."

"But I'm much better on land."

"I like you both ways." He pressed his faceplate against hers. "Kissing you."

"Right back," she said.

She pulled the basket up. He used an oversized toggle clip to attach it to his belt. "You go first."

She scrambled and gripped the line, using her shapely legs in those ridiculous pink flippers to propel herself up slowly, with the line as her guide. He was right beneath her.

Enjoying the view.

Noonan was babbling. He was dancing around the boat, stepping on things he was so excited. "Tell me what else you saw!"

Travis was drying off the lady of the ocean. "She's made of stone. Not wood. Stone."

"I know," said Noonan. "Listen, let's get her ashore. Travis, pull up the anchor, please."

Noonan began retracting the heavy anchor with the winch then checked with everyone. Ned was sorting through the rounded pieces of debris in the basket. He'd forgotten to remove his mask.

Madison tapped on the glass and then helped him remove it. "Now who's the fish, huh?"

"I remember once when I got a snorkel for my birthday. I slept with it on for a week," he said. "Funny, I'd forgotten that."

"Are we good to go?" Noonan shouted.

Ned gave him the thumbs-up. Then he pushed Travis back as he bent to examine the basket.

"No, son. You've already got a lot more to answer for first. We'll be fair, if there's anything. But you stay away now. You've breached the trust of the group."

Travis fell back into the seat and wrapped his arms around his torso again, without saying a word. Ned knew he was going to be a problem. He hoped that Noonan's friend had figured out a way they could go back and mine that wreck, but it wouldn't be with Travis.

The engines kicked in. Madison shared the pictures with Noonan as he piloted the boat down the coastline before he doubled back and headed North to Treasure Island.

It was still early afternoon, and Ned had searched the waters the whole way, not seeing another vessel until close to the pier. At the dock, Noonan ran to get a wagon they used to haul in catch on their fishing trips.

They loaded the lady, who was now wrapped in a blue tarp, onto the wagon. Ned carried the blackened pieces in his dive bag which he slung over his shoulders, leaving the basket behind on the boat. They greeted several older gentlemen sitting at the bar watching a baseball game. They passed through the outside of the club restaurant and into the parking lot. It took all four of them to load her into the back of Noonan's truck and closed the tailgate.

"No quick stops, Noonan, or she'll come flying out and take your tailgate with her." Ned laughed at how much it did look like he was hauling a dead body around.

"Okay, I'm off. I'll call you tomorrow as soon as I hear from my friend. Can you take Travis back?"

"Sure," said Madison. "You've earned a nice dinner, Travis. Thanks for your help."

"Nah, just drop me off on Gulf Boulevard. I've got plans."

Ned and Madison watched the young man walk sullenly down the road.

"Something doesn't feel right about that boy," Ned whispered.

"It's going to be a problem. But hey, you've got the pieces?"

"Oh fuck yes. I forgot all about them."

"Well, I'd say Noonan has all he can handle tonight. We'll return them to him tomorrow. I'm up for a nice dinner and a margarita. How about you?"

"Me too."

As she was pulling back onto Gulf Boulevard, he was thinking about that gallon of ice cream. It was going to taste very sweet tonight.

CHAPTER 18

Madison ordered the house *especial* margarita that was nearly as wide at the top as her fingers could spread. The frozen mixture gave her a brain freeze. She held her nose while Ned sat back in his seat, sipping his beer, laughing at her.

"For being a bartender, you don't seem to be able to deal with your liquor," he said playfully.

"I'm used to pouring drinks, not drinking them. Besides, it's an occupational hazard, and I tend to give alcohol a wide berth. Otherwise, I'd fall overboard like so many other bartenders who get hooked by the demon. And then they get fired. They're worthless."

"I've known one or two of those," he nodded.

She leaned into the table, knowing that the top of her tank gaped open for his benefit. It only took seconds before he noticed.

"You know, one thing is a mystery to me," she started.

"Mystery? What mystery?" His steady eyes bored into hers between their slow scanning.

The several sips of margarita began making her head fuzzy and hoped their food arrived soon. "You hung out with some pretty crusty dudes. You have seen so much in the world—more than I ever will."

"That's a fact, and I hope it will always stay that way, Madison."

"But how come it didn't taint you?"

He shook his head and then shrugged. "No idea. I haven't a fuckin' clue."

"When I first met you, I thought you were too much of a Boy Scout," she added.

He leaned into her, his lips inches from hers. "I am a Boy Scout. Through and through. I'm a force for good. I save the day. But I'm completely smitten by a mermaid." He kissed her.

She explored his face, the crease at the side of his full, sexy lips and the way his hair curled a little too long over his ears. His long lashes and warm brown eyes made her heart race.

"You're quite a package, I'll admit." After another kiss, she said, "I always liked the bad boys, the ones that were rough around the edges, maybe a little unfair, or didn't always do the right things. I liked finding their good parts, their soft parts. That was always the fun of it, because I feel deep inside everyone wants to be good and whole and to be honorable."

"You've found my soft parts, Maddie."

"Yes." She felt her cheeks turn pink.

He picked up her hand and kissed her palm. She loved that he did this often. It wasn't the back of her hand or her fingers. It was her palm, the warm underside of her heart that he kissed. "I was in hiding until you came along. Getting too close was something I always feared, in the romantic sense, that is. I loved my mother, and I guess I loved my dad, and they loved me back, or did the best they could. But I don't think I ever saw this."

"What?"

"What we have. I never saw my parents look at each other the way you and I do. I guess I thought it was all fake, something you'd see in the movies. My *Operator Brain,* as they call it on the Teams, was dominant. It would survive even though I would see unspeakable horror and disappointment. Like I was floating above it. Waiting. For you."

"So I did recover something inside you."

"Oh you definitely did that, Madison."

She laid her palms against his cheeks. "Damn you, Ned Silver, now I'll never be able to kiss another man again. You better not break my heart, because then I'd have to kill you!" she said between her tears.

He slipped off his chair and came to a kneel, holding her with his big arms wrapped around her waist and back, letting her head rest on the concrete that was his right shoulder.

When he released her, he said, "I don't want you to ever kiss another man, to ever look at another man for the rest of your life." He lowered his forehead, pointed two fingers in her direction, and then aimed at his own eyes. "You and me, together. You'll never be safer, Maddie. You let me fight the wars, and you keep stoking the fires when I come home. That's the way it's supposed to work."

"Is that fifty-fifty?"

He sat back in his chair. "You do remember that little thing I told you the other night. The part about lying back and letting a slow quiet man rock your world? I am that man, Maddie. That's all I want to do. It's dumb. There are lots of logical reasons why I shouldn't feel this way, but I do."

"I thought you were being overbearing."

"Because you knew I was right, didn't you?"

She glanced down at her toes. "No." But she started to smile anyway.

He laughed. "I watched your expression, and do you know what I saw?"

"I couldn't possibly imagine. Humor me." She put her chin in her palm, elbow on the table.

"I saw fear at first, because I figured you'd never

had that. And that's when I knew I could be that man for you. I just knew I'd have to bide my time, but you would belong to me one day."

He was right.

He slid his chair over. "Here, let me help you finish your drink, and then let's get the hell out of here."

"No dinner?"

"We have ice cream, remember?"

Her ears buzzed as he helped her into her car and prepared to take over the driving. Their waitress ran after them with their dinner order wrapped in a white plastic bag. Ned took the order, passing it over to her to hold, and handed the waitress some cash.

"Gracias, senor. Have a good evening," she said in her clipped English.

AT NED'S DOOR sat the stray dog, who barked at them when they drove up.

"Hey there, buddy," he said, as he knelt down and extended his hand. The dog was hesitant at first but finally got close enough to make a lunge, quickly licked his hand, and then sit back down.

"Speaking of being claimed, I think you've made a lifelong friend," she said. It touched her how tender Ned had been to this stray. "You should give him a bath when he's ready for it, and let him sleep inside. I don't mind dogs at all."

"He's not quite ready, I don't think. But let's see if he'll come inside. I'll get his food."

Once he opened the door and stepped back, the dog slipped past him and then sat by the outside door across the living room.

Madison put the food on the small table, lighting the candle there. Ned fixed some mixture of kibbles and wet food, opened the door, letting the dog out, and placed it down on the patio for him. The animal gulped it down like he had done before.

"That's amazing," Ned said to the glass, watching him eat.

Madison came up behind him, covering his backside with her front side. "They say strays always pick the best humans. I think he's a very smart dog. What are you going to call him?"

Ned inhaled sharply. He turned, holding his arm around her waist. "Otis. I think I'll call him Otis."

THE FOOD WENT largely untouched. They took turns feeding each other until the passion of their bodies took over, making concentrating on anything else an impossibility. As was his custom, he picked her up and brought her into the bedroom. He shed her clothes, peeling them off carefully, until she was left naked on the bed.

"I'll be right back!" he said as he removed his

clothes and left the room.

Maddie quickly got the pendant from the tiny pouch she kept in her purse and put it around her neck. She lay back down on the pillow, waiting for him.

Light showed from the kitchen and then got closer as she saw him at the doorway with the lit candle in one hand and the ice cream in the other. Out of the top of the carton was one large spoon.

Placing the candle on the bedside table, he lit the second candle. His eyes flashed in the warm light of the flame. Her breathing was hitched as she mused what he was up to.

"I want to see all of you," he whispered.

She sat up, leaning against his pillows as he climbed on the bed with the ice cream.

"Look what she put on for me," he said, fingering the pendant and then squeezing one breast.

"I thought you'd like it."

"I do, sweetheart. I surely do."

She followed his deliberate scoop, the muscles in his arm flexing deliciously. He held the spoon to her mouth, and she licked the tasty cream. He rubbed the back of the spoon over her lips as he licked his. She watched his eyes intently as he followed the rise and fall of her belly. She felt her body begin to flutter away, nearly on the edge of orgasm, without him doing anything but feed her ice cream.

The cool back of the spoon smoothed over her nipples, first the right one and then the left.

She closed her eyes and moaned. She felt the spoon travel down her abdomen, linger on her bellybutton, and then travel farther, leaving a trail of melted ice cream. She kept her eyes closed as he journeyed to the lips of her sex and rubbed the spoon against her, drenching them in the cold cream.

Next she felt his warm lips and tongue drinking the juices, sucking and lapping the ice cream off her tender parts, kissing her bellybutton, laving over both nipples. And then, slowly, she heard the spoon and the carton drop to the side on the floor as he mounted her, rubbed his cock up and down her dripping sex, and then thrust deep inside.

Her eyes flashed open. His face showed exactly what she was feeling, the ecstasy of their joining. The gentle rocking motion of his hips back and forth began a slow ride she never would tire of. The more he gave her, the more she wanted of him.

He'd talked about a quiet, slow man who could take control and rock her world. His sweet lovemaking melted whatever resistance and doubt she had. She had found her lifeline—her dive line. The way to Heaven itself.

CHAPTER 19

IN THE MORNING, Ned cleaned up the spilled ice cream quietly, letting Madison sleep. He slipped on his American flag boxers and made coffee then went outside to watch the sunrise. Starting his day by staring out at the ocean over a deserted white sand beach definitely changed his whole focus. Even in San Diego, where the beaches and blue sky and weather were all beautiful, there was traffic. It was a city. In Coronado, where they'd worked out, tourists watched as they phased through parts of BUD/S. His condo was above the skyline, but it took a half hour before he'd see any real big patch of blue water or beach.

This really was like paradise. He understood how it had changed his father. He understood why, when his dad went back to California that he could never quite get back here, and Ned understood more than ever why his father was so angry and sullen. He hadn't belonged there. He'd belonged here.

Ned wondered if he'd never met Madison if he would feel the same way, and he guessed he would. It was that one slice of Heaven he'd never allowed himself to taste. Everything about being alive was sweeter. He was tired of the gritty, dusty, and dirty parts of the world.

He was thinking about Madison's offer to have him move in with her. Caressing her nude body all night long, not being able to keep his hands off her, and waking up so damned sleep-deprived and ragged were exactly how he wanted to feel all the time. It was the kind of excess that was natural and right. It was truth and beauty. Once this whole thing with Noonan was put to bed, he'd sit down and talk with Madison, and if he didn't get so damned distracted with how her lips moved, how she ate ice cream, how she drank her coffee, and how she felt in the warm shower beneath his fingers, he could design a life the two of them could share.

It's a fuckin' good problem to have.

Within minutes, Otis found his way from wherever he'd been sleeping and curled up at his feet. Ned leaned over and was able to pet the dog.

"You want some breakfast, Otis?"

The dog cracked his head, one ear arching up, indicating he knew what the word food meant.

Ned made him another mixture, leaving the door

ajar. Otis sat quietly on the other side, waiting. He grabbed the bowl and was headed outside when his cell buzzed, nearly bouncing off the kitchen counter. It was his mom. He picked it up, cupped it between his ear and shoulder, poured himself another cup of coffee, and took the food out to Otis, closing the door behind him.

"Hello, Mom. How is everything? How'd it go with Flo?"

"Better than I expected. She seems to have calmed down. It's less upsetting to have her in one place, for her, as well as everyone else. I think she'll like it there."

"That's good news. I've been thinking about you and hoping it was going okay. And you? You holding up?" Ned knew she would still hold a bit of guilt about sending her sister to the home.

"I'm adjusting to being alone now. Didn't realize how much of my time it took to take care of your dad and to shuttle Flo around everywhere. Haven't gotten used to it yet."

The slight negativity in her voice worried him.

"Nobody expects this to be easy. Such big changes. I think you're doing a way better job than you give yourself credit for." He hesitated but then added, "And I know how you loved dad. I can see that now."

"Thank you, Ned." He could tell she was beginning to cry.

"I shouldn't have said it. I made you sad."

"No, it's just nice to hear it. I never wanted the two of you to be so distant. You weren't when you were young."

"Funny you should say that. I was just telling Mad—I was just talking yesterday about him. Remember when you bought that snorkel mask and I wouldn't sleep without it for a week?"

She laughed. "I do. Your dad thought that was so funny. He bought that for you for your birthday. It touched him that you wanted to snorkel like he did."

"I've been recalling some of those times, Mom. Some of them have come back to me. I don't know why it changed."

"He never could stop drinking. I used to call him the King of Good Times. The party animal that he was, he could never find solace without the alcohol. It was a shame to watch it destroy everything he loved. You know, he used to talk about taking me to Florida, but after he got so bad, he didn't want to go any longer."

Ned felt his mother's heartache. Felt for the life they could have had. "I love you, Mom."

"And you were the joy of my life, Ned. The real love of my life. Honest."

He watched the gentle waves undulate while he waited for her to continue. He wasn't sure where he should go with this honest reveal.

"How about you?" she asked, finally.

He leaned back against the chair and checked out the sky. That was a big, long question. How could he tell his mom that his whole life had changed, that there was something else bigger out there for him now?

"I'm on an adventure, for sure. I love this place and everything about it. Old Noonan is a character, and I've met some other salty characters." He felt his voice lower and get husky. "And some lovely girls."

"Ah, well, that's good for you."

"Yes, it is."

"Is he anything like your father?"

"Who? Noonan? No way. I mean in some things, yes. I could see how they liked to do things together, especially drink, you know. But Noonan has a pretty good gig here, out on the water, taking people diving. It's a nice lifestyle. Pretty colors, white sand beach, and turquoise water that's crystal clear to swim in. I can see why Dad liked it."

"Now I wish I'd gone."

"You've never been? You might have stayed out here if you'd come."

"I made another choice. I had to be the one he came back to. That was important to me. Later, well, maybe I waited too long and should have encouraged it. Maybe it would have been better for us. But back then, it wasn't right for me to follow him around. He had to want to come home. I never begrudged him his trip. I guess it was his last taste of freedom."

"You were pregnant, weren't you? Don't answer that if you don't want to."

"I think you knew all along it was that way. But we were married. It all happened so fast."

There was another pause. Ned watched a pelican dive into the ocean and come up with a wiggling fish it inhaled as it floated in the glassy blue water.

"Maybe you should come out here some day and look around. I'm beginning to feel like I was meant to be here, Mom. I really was."

"That sounds like you've met someone. Does Noonan know?"

"That's how I met her."

His mother was quiet. Then she sighed. "Old Noonan. Your dad idolized him, wanted to be just like him. Always looking for that one big deal to make him rich."

Ned laughed. "He's still doing that."

"He never had any money, your dad said. We bought a house, had a car, and went on trips. Noonan, he said, just lived like a beach bum. He gave up everything. Never had a family. It's funny how two friends can both envy the life of the other."

Ned had never thought about that before. Noonan had remained a rolling stone. His dad got the good jobs, until he became too unreliable to hold down one, and had the wife and child. He got to be the Coach and live through the eyes of his son, be part of a community. Noonan had his freedom. And he had a dream. Pirate Jake had buried his.

"Well, just give it a thought. I'd be happy to show you around here. Give yourself permission to heal, Mom. You deserve it."

"Thank you, Ned. I will. Does this mean you're not returning?"

Had he said that? Is that what he meant?

"No, I'm not there yet. But trust me, you need to see this place. It is paradise. I think it would change your whole life."

He signed off with his mom without telling her specifically about Madison, deciding to do that later.

Otis had finished his food and disappeared around the corner.

Ned wondered if his mother had ever read that little book of poetry. He guessed that she hadn't, that she'd given him the space to have his secret. And, if she didn't know, she wouldn't have to wonder. At the right time and place, he wanted to let Madison read that beautiful piece someone had written, the one his dad liked. And see the picture of the vagabond group of hippies and beatniks who had found themselves at Treasure Island.

One thing at a time. A few pieces had to drop into place, first.

The next call Ned got was from Noonan.

"What's up?"

"Trouble."

Ned sat up. "What happened?"

"I need to come over. Can I?"

"Sure. When?"

"Now."

"Okay. I've got Madison still sleeping, but I can fix you breakfast if you're hungry."

"I'll be right over." Noonan disconnected before Ned could ask anything more.

He opened the door to the bedroom quietly and saw her lying on her back, her long hair strewn over his pillow, her arms up over her head and her legs entangled in the sheets they'd completely rearranged last night. Between her breasts she still wore the mermaid pendant. From the waist up, her form was one of a statue like the one they'd found. Her breasts were full and perfectly round, larger than his hand could manage no matter how hard he tried. Her nipples were soft and inviting.

Her eyes opened slowly.

"You were awake already?"

She arched, stretching her long arms, and gave him a crooked smile. "Not telling."

He sat on the edge of the bed. She wrapped her arms around his waist and begged him to join her.

"I can't. Noonan is coming over. Something's wrong. You're going to need to get dressed quickly, okay?"

She sat up, keeping the sheet across her chest. "That sounds bad."

"I hope not," he said as he pulled the sheet down. "I had all kind of plans for today."

"Ice cream?"

He shook his head. "Sorry, the ice cream is all gone. But trust me, we'll get more."

"You better."

She got up and slipped into the bra and panties that lay on the floor where Ned had left them last night. She threw the tank top over her head and pulled up her jeans. She stopped.

"Ned? You're standing in your shorts. Aren't you going to get dressed too?"

It jolted him back to the reality of what their morning would be like. "Yup, so sorry. I was overcome with your beauty."

Madison helped him crack eggs. Ned put spinach and cheese into the mixture, cooked toast, and made more coffee. They heard a knock at the front door.

Noonan came barging in. The front side of his shirt was covered in blood, and on his knees were two dark red stains. His eyes were wild. Ned looked outside and saw the tarp still in the back of his pickup truck and then closed the door. Madison brought him a towel.

"Is this you?" she asked as she pulled off his shirt, examining his chest and back.

"No. My buddy, Gary. I found him at home this morning. His throat had been cut. Like a dumbass, I thought I could help him. But he was already dead several hours."

"Did you call the police?"

"Not yet."

"Shit, Noonan, you should have done that right away. Got your phone?"

Noonan pulled it out of his pocket and held it above his head. "Wait a minute. Hear me out first."

Madison pulled on Noonan's jeans, causing his cell phone to fall to the floor, which Ned grabbed and returned to him. "I'm washing these too." She started to take them away. "Ned, do you have a washer?"

"It's in the garage."

Noonan was standing in a navy blue pair of mid-thigh free rangers. He crossed his arms as if giving his tits privacy and looked ridiculous.

Madison returned from the garage. Noonan hand-ed her the bloody towel. "Better put this in there too."

"Come on. Let's get you cleaned up before I have you sitting down on anything."

As he passed by the door to the beach, he spotted the dog. "You got a dog?" he asked.

"No, the dog got *me*. Now get in here, Noonan." He dragged the man into the bathroom and turned on the shower. He shoved lemon shower gel into his belly. "Strip and wash."

The pirate took off his undies and tossed them behind Ned.

"There's a towel on the toilet seat for you."

Madison took the underwear with her nose up-turned, holding it by her thumb and forefinger. When she came back, she poured the egg mixture into the frying pan and started to make the scramble. Then she buttered the now-cold toast.

"Did he say anything?" she asked as Ned made orange juice.

"Not yet. I'm going to strangle that little shit Travis if he's involved in this."

Noonan waddled out with the towel around his waist and collapsed into the couch. He looked in shock.

Ned handed him a glass of orange juice.

"Better start spilling or I'm calling the cops myself."

"Gary, that's my buddy, and I had a conversation last night. When I told him what I'd found, he told me to hang onto it and not to talk to anyone. He said he had some feelers out to a couple crews, you know, people he could trust. They were interested and wanted to see pictures. So he planned to go down to the survey office this morning and poke around. We were to meet at T.J.'s about five last night so I could show him the statue and the pictures. He never showed. I called him a dozen times."

Noonan laced his fingers through his hair and leaned over his towel-clad knees.

"You should have called me, Noonan."

"Well, Gary does get smashed now and then. I just thought he holed up somewhere. But when I couldn't get him this morning, I started to worry."

"Drink some juice, Noonan. You want coffee?"

"No. No coffee. My nerves are shot already. Look at this." He held his hand up, and Ned could see how badly he shook.

"Take the juice. So where was he? How did you find him?"

"He has a little place over on West Eighth, has a girlfriend there. He's been staying with her sometimes and now is watching her fish while she's on a cruise." Noonan rolled his eyes and drank down his orange juice.

"I found him just inside the front door, which had been kicked open. They ransacked the house too, pulled everything out of the shelves, drawers in the bedroom, kitchen."

"Was he tortured?" Ned asked calmly.

"What?"

"Cigarette burns on his chest, cuts? Little finger clipped?"

Madison reacted, putting her hands over her ears.

Noonan was thinking, turning his head from side to side, trying to recall.

"Come on, Noonan. It's important."

"His mouth. He had blood coming from his mouth. Oh, and I remember now, they'd knocked one of his teeth out and it was lying beside his head."

"No, they *pulled* it out, Noonan. That's what they do."

"Shit."

Ned knew that all of them were now known to whoever wanted to get Noonan's buddy. "Did you go back to your place?"

"No. Last night I went to my sister's in Sarasota. I got spooked when he didn't show up."

"Did Travis know about this guy?"

"Sure. We had dinner together a couple of times. Travis loves the stories."

"Then don't go back to your place. Do you think they know where I'm staying?"

"You don't think—"

"Shut up, Noonan. They were looking for information. What did you tell Gary? I need to know everything."

Madison brought him a plate of eggs. Ned waived his off. Noonan ate nervously.

Before Noonan began, Ned had another idea. "Give me your keys."

"Oh fuck, I left them in my pants."

"Not to worry," said Madison, who went to the garage and retrieved them.

"I'm parking your truck in my garage so no one can see it. Hard to mistake that turquoise truck with a pirate painted on the door."

"They'd go to the boat. Oh God! You don't think they'd mess with my boat?"

As he left the house, he called back. "At this point, we're trying to protect your life. You can always get another boat."

He opened the garage door then pulled Noonan's truck inside. He poked his head out onto the alleyway, didn't see anyone watching, and hit the remote. Judging from the angle to Gulf Boulevard, he doubted anyone would have seen it passing by there, either.

He dropped the keys on the counter.

"Now, you tell me what information you gave Gary, because whatever he knows, they know too."

"I told him we found the lady. I figured it would do no harm. I asked him not to tell the crews about it, because the statue was distinctive. I told him I had pictures I could show whomever. He wanted to see them, so he could verify that he had. They'd ask him this."

"Does he know we were diving at the barge?"

"Yes, of course. I told him that's how we discovered it."

"Then they know where to look."

"So no one has checked the survey office, then?" asked Madison.

"I don't think Gary ever made it. He'd been dead awhile."

"They'd look for Noonan at the Salty Dog," gasped Madison. "Should I call in?"

"Not yet." Ned hated to do it, but he had to be honest with Noonan. "I think we have to face the fact that we're outmatched. We have proof of the find. We might be able to confirm we were out there. But the biggest problem is someone's trying to get information, and maybe they have it now if they checked the tax office. They'd see you got a permit, right?"

"Yes, they would."

"We have to involve the police. For your safety."

"But, Ned, that means we have to give up the find."

"I hope not. But, Noonan, they're going to kill you if they don't get what they want. I'm sure they know about you from Travis. That means they know about me and Madison. I can't fight all that by myself."

"Should I call Travis?" asked Madison.

Ned didn't want to tell them, but it was best. "I don't think Travis cares any longer. I'm pretty sure no one will find him now."

CHAPTER 20

MADISON WONDERED ABOUT her mother and whether or not she was safe. Ned was going to take Noonan down to the Treasure Island Police Department, now that his clothes were clean and dry. They moved the wrapped statue to Ned's garage until they could sort everything out.

She'd met several of the local police and fire regulars at the Salty Dog over the years, and they were a decent bunch of guys. She told Ned. But one thing still bothered her.

"Ned, I need to check in with Monty. He's called like three times this morning. I think he expects me to come in."

"I'd prefer you didn't."

Noonan piped up. "Ned, I think she'd be a helluva lot safer there than at her place alone. Just until we get finished."

"I could come with you, but what would be the

point? At the Dog, at least I'm doing something. There would be lots of eyes on me."

She could tell he was reluctant, but in the end, he agreed.

"You have an extra tee shirt I could borrow?" she asked.

"Of course I do."

She pulled off her tank top and donned his SEAL Team 3 grey shirt with the navy blue and gold Team logo. He touched the mermaid pendant.

"You wear that thing inside. Don't show it to anyone, understood?"

"I got it."

"Hey, Ned, did you take the rocks, the ones you said pinged for possible silver?"

"They're in my dive pack."

"Let's bring them. We can show those, I just don't want to say anything about the lady of the ocean."

"I should call Mom and give her a heads-up."

"She'd kick your butt if she found out later you didn't," barked Noonan. "Your funeral."

Ned laughed. "Now I know where you get all that fire, Madison."

"Got that right," said Noonan.

He smiled again, his hands placed at her shoulders. "Get straight to work, honey. We'll follow you down as far as the police station, but you go straight to work.

You can call her there, okay?"

"Okay. Let me know how it goes."

"Will do."

She followed Noonan's truck down Gulf Boulevard. Occasionally she let another car slip in between them, but no one appeared especially interested in the two men in the turquoise vehicle.

When they pulled into the parking lot of the City complex, she remained heading North and in less than ten minutes was at the Salty Dog.

Stepping through the doorway, she felt like she was coming back home after a long vacation, instead of only three days away. But so much had changed. Behind the bar, she found the beer had been left unstocked. Dirty dishes were piled in the sink so she set them aside and hand-washed nearly two dozen glasses, leaving them to air dry on a towel on the counter. She had never seen it left in such a disorganized and dirty condition before.

Iris arrived an hour late, frosty as ever. "Well, look at what the cat dragged in. Old Garrison was heartsick, missing you. He'll be glad you're back."

"It's nice to be missed," she said with a cool stare to Iris' back.

Without offering explanation or helping to clean up, Iris greeted the next couple who came in and took her first order.

Cook Jones exited his kingdom, presenting Madison with his specialty—jambalaya, which he knew to be her favorite. "Don't go kissing anybody for a few hours, or their lips will swell up and look like mine!" He grinned, proud of his concoction.

"Oh, bless your soul, Washington Jones. Just what I needed!"

The warm soup was just the right kind of spicy, and after a few sips Madison went back to her cleaning. She wiped down the counters and all the tables, which had also been ignored.

She told Iris she had to make a phone call, brought her jambalaya to one of the tables in the corner and dialed Monty first.

"Where the hell have you been?"

"I told you three days, Monty. I was gone for three days. I'm here now. Got here before Iris."

"Thank God. It was a mess last night. I had to bring in one of Jones' boys severance, and stayed until closing, and even then we didn't finish everything."

"I noticed. I've taken care of the tables and the glasses. Anything else?"

"The beer bottles—"

"Are already done."

"You have a nice vacation?"

She smiled to herself. "You could say that."

"You had some visitors in here last night asking

about you and Noonan."

"Oh?" Madison's pulse quickened.

"Yeah, a couple. She said she went to school with you."

"Who were they? What did they look like?"

"To be honest, it was dark and we were kind of busy. She acted like she was a friend. Your mother was here, so I told them to go speak to her."

"You did what?"

"Just a friendly chat."

"What happened to my mom?"

"Nothing. They just chatted. Your mom finished her dinner and left. She was in a fine mood. I think she was looking for Noonan."

"Where did the couple go?"

"They'd already gone by the time your mom left. I think they're coming over tonight, or so she said."

Madison could hardly breathe. The next person she called was her mother, but she didn't get an answer.

She dialed Ned.

"We're in the interview room. I'll have to call you back."

"No, hear me out. Some people came in here last night looking for us, and Monty had them talk to my mother. Now she doesn't answer, Ned. I'm worried."

"You stay there."

"Not on your life. I'm going to check on her."

"Not alone, Madison." She heard him excuse himself and then he continued, "We're going to be here for an hour or more. Then I'll come get you."

"I need to make sure she's okay."

"You stay safe. Don't go anywhere."

"But—"

"I'll break away and come get you soon. Madison, I have to know you're safe."

She didn't want to promise Ned, but in the end, she did. During the next half hour, she tried to call her mother six times, never getting an answer. Madison wondered if she was going through one of her inspirational moods where she switched off everything electronic except her coffee maker.

Then her mother called.

"Oh my God, Mom. I tried calling you like twenty times."

"Maddie, can you come over?"

She sounded like she'd been crying.

"Mom? Are you okay?"

"Just come over."

The call disconnected.

Madison tried to call back but her mother didn't pick up. Then she dialed Ned, but his phone went right to voicemail. She also tried Noonan, with the same result.

She called the Treasure Island Police Department

and got a recorded line with a promise of a returned call within thirty minutes. The recording went into, "If this is an emergency, hang up and dial 9-1-1."

She knew she shouldn't do it, but her mother needed her. Maddie had promised. Her mother wouldn't ask unless it was important.

She threw down her towel, grabbed her purse and headed to her car.

CHAPTER 21

"**W**E'VE ALREADY TOLD you several times. Look, we have a few items we brought up from the dive. Gary was supposed to contact a couple of reputable crews to see about going forward," Noonan boomed.

The interview room was hot. Ned knew they'd be separated soon if they really suspected Noonan being complicit in the murder of his friend. He'd get his hour or two, and Noonan would probably wind up being here the whole day. He checked his phone and saw several calls from Madison, and that worried him.

"You wanna tell us why you're checking your phone so much?" asked one of the detectives. "As a matter of fact, can I please look at your phone for a minute?"

Ned had nothing at all to hide. But he hadn't played the Navy SEAL card yet, either.

"Sorry, but I got classified numbers on here. I'm an

active duty Navy SEAL, and I can give you my credentials, if you like, since you didn't ask for them."

He reached into his back pocket and provided his California Driver's license and his military I.D. It seemed to give him some space. The detective's eyebrows rose.

"What brings you out to Florida? You do treasure hunting too in your spare time?"

"As he's told you, Noonan got a contract to do this dive. My dad and Noonan served in the Navy together. And he's just passed. I came out here to see Dad's old friend here, and visit some of my dad's haunts."

The detective checked with his partner, who nodded. He returned his cards. "Thank you for your service, son."

"I'm lucky to do it, sir." Ned added, "And as to your question about my phone calls, my girlfriend is worried about her mother, who apparently had a conversation with individuals last night asking for Noonan. She's not been able to speak to her since."

"Oh shit," Noonan whispered, covering his face.

"When did you find out about this?" the larger detective asked him.

"Just now. She called me. Now she's calling me back and I gotta take these calls."

"Mr. Silver, you can step outside and make your calls. Noonan, I'm going to ask you to stay behind just for a few more minutes."

Ned was shown to the lobby by one of the detectives, who identified himself as Wade Corrigan. "Listen, I've known Noonan since I was a kid, and I don't suspect him of anything. And everyone knows around here that he's just a good old guy. We have a new police chief, hired from outside our state, and I just need to make sure there are no holes or I'll get my ass chewed. Make your calls, and then I need to talk to you about something."

"Sure thing."

Ned rang Madison. It rang and then went to voicemail. "Shit."

"Well, keep trying. I'm sorry about all this. You want me to run you over to her mom's?"

"That's just it, I don't have the address. Never been there."

"And Noonan?"

"Oh yeah, he knows. He'd have to come with us. Can we make this happen?"

"Let's go do it, son."

Even though the big detective was only about ten years older than Ned, he placed his hand on his shoulder and showed him the way back to the hallway and knocked on the door.

"Hey there, we're gonna let him go, aren't we?" he asked the other detective.

"I'm thinking yes. I've got to go over to the crime scene again."

"Listen, I'm gonna give Mr. Silver an escort to the mother's house. I need Noonan to give me the address."

"No, I want to come," yelled Noonan. "I need to be there."

Ned had to say something. "Fellas, time's wasting. Send him over in a patrol car if you have to, but let's get some speed on this mission."

"Very well. We can do that. You ride with Corrigan. I'll get a patrol unit out front. He can get us there faster."

"I'll call you," Corrigan motioned to his partner.

"Thanks, fellas," said Noonan, shaking hands.

Seconds later, Ned was seated next to Detective Corrigan, speeding behind the flashing patrol car headed North. At this rate, it wouldn't take more than a few minutes for them to arrive.

"You know this Travis Hicks kid very well?" Corrigan asked him.

"Noonan used to use him on dives. I didn't know him at all. But we think he's the one who had the connection to the folks who were involved with the murder. And now that someone's come to the Salty Dog, I'm sure of it."

"He's been in and out of juvie since he was ten. Not

supposed to tell you that. We found him out at the dock. Apparently he slept on the Bones."

"Is he okay?"

"Not exactly. He also had an encounter with a knife while shaving."

Ned felt bad about the kid, even though he had put everyone in danger. "That's too bad. I think Noonan was way too trusting. Lived in kind of a fantasy."

"That's the thing out here. We're supposed to make it look like paradise all the time, but bad things happen. We're supposed to keep the bad guys away from the senior citizens, who sometimes haven't a clue what kind of danger they're in."

Ned felt the same way about his job.

"I get it. We do the same thing on the Teams. We go out there doing things so everyone can go crazy batshit over-spending, going to coffee, playing on the beach, and living it up. We both make it safe for their families. Neither one of us can talk about what we see, either."

"Absolutely. Wish I could stop the dreams, though."

"Me too, brother. Me too."

The patrol car took the turn toward the beach a little too quickly and sent up a huge dust cloud, but he managed to keep the car on the road. He left his lights on but turned off the siren.

The tiny house with bright flowered vines all along the front porch looked innocuous enough. But since Madison's car was there and she wasn't answering her cell, Ned's operator brain kicked in, and he was looking for options. One dark SUV was parked around the corner in the alleyway the police cars had just blocked off. It appeared to be vacant.

"I'm going to make my way around the side and see if I can look inside any of the windows."

"Look, we gotta do this the right way. I can't have you involved."

"But I'm trained—"

"No can do. You know the rules. We have to attempt to contact the occupants first."

"Who's going to do that?"

"He is," detective Corrigan said, nodding toward the red-headed patrolman, who was leading outside his patrol car, his weapon raised. Noonan was instructed to stay in the car when he tried to open his door. "He's the one with the bullet-proof vest."

Ned heard the scratchy instructions coming from the young policeman's shoulder microphone.

"You stay here," Corrigan whispered and drew his weapon holding it with both hands, aimed at the ground, following well behind the young officer.

Ned heard the young policeman yell, "This is the Treasure Island Police. Please exit the domicile with your hands up."

There was no answer. Ned's blood pressure soared.

"Anyone home?" the young policemen shouted. When he got no answer, he knocked on the front door with his fist. "We need you to come out with your hands up. This is Treasure Island Police. We need your cooperation."

His demand was met with a blast coming from inside the home, piercing the wooden front door and hitting the young officer in the chest.

CHAPTER 22

MADISON ARRIVED AT her mother's place, opening the front door without knocking. She walked into a living room full of people. Her mother was one of the five, the only one with her hands tied in front of her. Her clip had come out of her hair, and her large house dress was slung over one shoulder, like she'd been shoved down onto the couch and made to sit.

She was startled at first, but seeing her mother's eyes and the tears streaming down her face broke her heart.

"I'm so sorry, Maddie. They made me call you," she said as she shook her head.

Madison scanned the four strangers and didn't recognize any of them. They were young, hard-looking kids, the kind she wouldn't have wanted to serve at the Dog. The woman motioned to the young man next to her and he grabbed Madison by the forearm and plunked her down onto the couch next to her mother.

He pulled a thick zip tie from his back pocket and secured her hands together.

"We were hoping that would work out this way," said the woman, who sat across from them in an overstuffed chair. "So far so good."

"What do you want?" demanded Madison. "We don't have any money. Take whatever you like, but you can see, my house looks just like this one. We don't own anything of value. Why are you doing this?"

"Oh, don't play dumb with me. We're here for co-operation. We understand you're quite the looker. Oliver and Carlos here might want a little more private cooperation, nothing harmful, of course. We under-stand you've seen some treasure, and we want our fair share."

"What's your fair share?" Madison sneered.

"All of it."

When Madison scoffed, the woman continued. "You'd better consider this. Isn't it worth less than your lives? How about the life of your mother?"

One of the men tugged on her mother's hair, pull-ing her head back and placing a knife below her chin. Her mother cried out and Madison attempted to lunge for the woman but was yanked back by one of the other men. Both women were pushed back together onto the couch.

A tall, pockmarked youth who appeared not to be

older than a teen ducked his head and examined the action on the beach outside. He paced the room holding a rifle, sneering down at her.

"Oh God, Maddie, forgive me," her mother whispered.

"Shh!" said the woman. "What I want to know is where Mr. Noonan LaFontaine is. And I understand he has your boyfriend with him?"

Madison had to think quickly. She wasn't sure what to say. Her mother arched back at the word boyfriend.

"They went to the survey office, I think. Then they were going out today to do more exploring."

"Yes, that's what we're interested in. So where is the stuff you already brought up?" she asked.

That confirmed Travis had been the one who had given out the information. He was the only one, other than the dead man, who would know.

"He has them."

"Who?"

"Noonan. He has them in his dive pack."

"And what else did you find?"

"N-nothing. There were several rocks, about seven, eight rocks we brought up to have tested. Nothing conclusive."

"Then why go to the survey office?"

"To expand their claim. They have a permit to dive."

"Travis said you found a statue. Where is that stat-ue?"

Madison was stumped at first. "In the back of Noonan's truck, last time I saw."

"So you were going to meet up with them later on today?"

"Y-yes." She was delighted that apparently the woman didn't know the police had gotten involved.

"And what about the mermaid?"

"The what?" Madison asked.

"The necklace."

Madison exchanged a look with her mother and saw recognition in her eyes that her mother knew about the necklace.

"It's a copy. A fake. But it looks real."

"Give me a look at it."

Madison lowered her head, reached behind her neck, and unclasped the pendant. She was about to hand it over to the woman when her mother tried to touch it with her bound hands. "It's just an old trinket, something we got in St. Pete at one of the dive shops. Looks real, though." She could tell her mother was in shock.

"Here. If this is what you're looking for, knock yourself out. Go buy ice cream for your crew with the proceeds."

The woman grabbed the necklace and, with her

other hand, slapped Madison across her cheek. Her mother reacted in protest.

Both women watched as the team ogled over the naked mermaid as if she'd been violated by unclean hands. Madison knew it meant something to her mother, but whatever it was, it wasn't worth her life to try to get it back. Time was on her side. She decided to get into conversation.

"I'm not sure what you think is going on, but this dive is not a treasure dive. They're actually looking for a dog collar. I'm not sure what Travis told you, but we found the barge. Just a big box of a thing. Sunk over two hundred years ago. The dog collar was a necklace the barge's cook owned. It was a fake. The setting was platinum, but the stones were glass. There's a family in North Carolina who want it for sentimental reasons. Travis knew all that."

Madison could see she'd gotten the attention of one of the men, who frowned. "That little shit."

"She's lying, Oliver."

"Well, you can see for yourself. The permit says we're looking for a dog collar. It was just a funded three-day dive for wages. Not for loot."

"What about the old ship?" the woman asked.

Madison was getting into it now. Lying was getting easier. She was mimicking all the things she'd seen Noonan and his friends exaggerating about while they drank in the Dog. She'd heard the tales for years.

She wrinkled her nose. "There was no ship. Come on. Travis knows the difference between a barge and an old ship. The thing was square. It was carrying things from Cuba to some place along the Florida coast. Mostly molasses and stuff. We found broken pots and piles of old tools that had turned to red pudding. The statue was probably someone sending a sculpture for a garden. Who knows? But as far as treasure, I hope you didn't spend too much money on Travis. He took you for a ride."

"Yes, well, we took care of that."

Madison wanted to not show fear, but Ned had informed them already that Travis probably wasn't among the living. She tried one more tactic.

"Look, if you let my mom go, I'll stay with you guys, and I'll take you there myself."

"You know how to find it?"

"Yes, I do."

The woman stood. "We don't need her then," she said, pointing at Madison's mother.

Just then, they heard a siren close and then silence. A second later, someone shouted from outside, "Treasure Island Police. Open Up."

In slow motion, Madison grabbed for the knife above her mother's head and watched the shooter raise his rifle and blast through the front door.

CHAPTER 23

NED NEARLY TRIPPED on Noonan as he ran around the side of both cars to where the fallen officer lay. He was trying to get up, but the wind had been knocked out of him.

Ned quickly dragged him away into the bushes at the side of the house, not wanting to be the object of a second blast.

Screaming erupted inside the house, the unmistakable sound of Madison's pitch, but unlike anything he'd ever heard from her before. Things were crashing, and he also heard broken glass as someone either broke in or out of a window on the beach side.

He scanned the area. Both Noonan and the detective were gone.

Out from the splinters of the front door came the shooter, looking like a scared kid.

Ned yelled at him.

"You don't want to do that, Son!"

But the kid was panicking and slowly raising his rifle to take direct aim at Ned.

His operator brain kicked in. Like it was a part of his body, he pulled his KA-BAR out of its sheath and in one well-practiced move, threw it as hard as he could before the kid could take proper aim. It caught him near the clavicle, sinking into soft tissue there. The force of the blade knocked the boy back, and he dropped his rifle.

Ned bolted, kicking the weapon to the side, but his target was completely overtaken by the shock of that huge knife handle sticking outside his chest. Blood was spurting over his chin, spilling down his torso and onto the ground.

Ned burst inside, where it had gotten quiet all of a sudden.

He was trained to look for a weapon first and then for blood. He found both immediately. Madison was holding a bloody boning knife, her arm also covered in crimson streaks. A man had fallen against the wall, leaving bloody smudge marks behind him, immobilized and dazed. Noonan had tackled a woman and had dislocated her shoulder. Her white face showed the agony she was in as she moaned. Detective Corrigan was placing a zip tie on one man, sitting on another who appeared unconscious.

But then he looked back at Madison. Her shocked

expression wasn't nearly as profound as the expression from the woman in front of her, an attractive grey-haired lady who must have been Madison's mother. She stared at Ned like she'd seen a ghost.

"Jake?" she called out.

Ned thought she was crazy, driven mad by the circumstances they were in.

"Jake! You came back!" she said again.

Ned looked around, hoping to find someone else standing there, but she was addressing him.

"No, Jake's my dad. I'm Ned."

The woman fainted.

A flurry of police cars arrived and neighbors began piling out from their beach bungalows, wearing bathing suits, flip flops, and straw sun hats. A couple of the onlookers were drinking cocktails.

Ned approached Madison, and she collapsed into him.

"Hey, Madison, let me take this, okay?" he said as he carefully unpeeled the knife from her fingers. He was thinking she looked like the day he'd gone hunting with his father and killed his first rabbit. It was too late to regret not taking the animal's life. Madison was still processing what she'd just done. Glancing over at the man leaning against the wall with a stab wound in his chest, Ned noticed he was still moving, and was grateful.

"You did real good, Madison. You didn't kill him."

She frowned as if seeing him for the first time and didn't know who he was. "But I wanted to. He was going to kill my mother."

At the sound of her daughter's voice, her mother sat up, dazed, but apparently unhurt.

Police were filing in. The detective brought Ned his KA-BAR, wiping it on the jacket of the woman Noonan had tackled and subdued. "You dropped this."

"Thanks, man."

He sat Madison down, worried she would be going into shock at any second. He sheathed his knife and noticed the pendant in the fingers of the groaning woman on the floor. He picked it up, rubbed the silver mermaid clean, and placed it in Madison's hands, curling her fingers over it just like his mother had done when she presented it to Ned.

"This is yours now."

Her mother blinked several times, having watched him hand her daughter the pendant.

"Maddie? Explain this to me."

Madison uncoiled her fingers and touched the curves of the silver mermaid. Ned saw that she began to piece together what had just occurred. "This is mine, Mom. Ned gave it to me. He got it from his father, Jake. Mom, this is the man I love, Ned Silver."

"THE MAN YOU love? You said the man you love?"

"I did say that?" Maddie smiled up to him in the shower. Her slippery body gliding past his filled him with joy. He wasn't sure it would come back so fast.

"I liked hearing it. Of course, I never expected to hear it from some crazy woman, covered in blood and holding an eight inch serrated blade. That's a lethal weapon."

Madison nodded her head and looked down at her toes. Water sluiced over them both. The shower smelled of lemons. All the blood was gone. Ned had inspected every part of her and found nothing scratched, bleeding or bruised. He'd tickled her while he was doing it, too. Her warm psyche came back, which was what he'd been most worried about.

The police had detained them just for a few minutes and then let them slip away in Maddie's car. Noonan took charge of her mother, since both of them were going to the hospital to be checked. The ordeal had left her mother short of breath, and Noonan thought he might have cracked a couple of ribs.

The young red-haired officer showed Ned the three-inch bruise that was forming in the middle of his chest, just before he put Maddie in the car and drove her home. To his place.

All the remnants of the danger had been washed away. He'd massaged her neck and shoulders, working her into putty. He said wanted her to sleep, told her she should go to bed and just rest until tomorrow so everything could settle down inside her.

She nodded agreement as he dried her off. Yet she leaned into him while he dried himself off. He picked her up and brought her into the bedroom. At the back door, Otis sat. He stopped.

"You're going to have to be patient. You'll get fed later," he said to the dog, who turned his head and flipped one ear up over the other.

"That's not fair. You should feed him. I'll be fine."

He kissed her then lay her on the bed. She immediately passed out.

He prepared kibble and meat for Otis and brought him a fresh bowl of water as well. He sat down on the patio chair and watched as the late afternoon sun hung in the sky. The sounds of the ocean and normal life soothed him. Even the sounds of Otis chowing down was a welcomed noise.

He pulled the pendant from his jeans and brushed over the curves in the mermaid. Madison had taken it off for the shower, but he knew the only place for her to be was around her neck.

He thought about coming out at sunset to watch like all the others did on Treasure Island, like people did in little towns all up and down the peninsula along the Gulf. It was a ritual, a healing ritual, he thought.

He watched Otis scamper around the corner again and disappear. Ned walked back inside, went to the bedroom, and studied Madison sleeping, her arms out to the sides, her long blonde hair streaking across the bed.

She's the real mermaid. She's the one my father hoped I'd find.

Gently, he put the chain around her neck and clasped it, marveling how it looked balanced between her two beautiful breasts.

The necklace belonged to Madison.

And Madison was his.

CHAPTER 24

MADISON GOT A week off after the rescue. Her boss was just grateful that, when Ned went back to California, she'd agreed to work behind the bar at the Salty Dog.

Noonan was able to partner with a large salvage operation, who had a team of attorneys all over the survey filing, and had the tax office issue a new warrant for additional finds. They were estimating the find to be significant. Noonan was finally able to embrace the possibility he could wind up a rich man. But not even that could tempt Madison or Ned to go back out into the water and hunt for treasure.

They spent lazy days and nights in bed—going to bed late, walking the beach at sunset, and waking up early to catch the sunrise. Otis began walking with them during these beach forays, or sat beside them on the blanket while they basked in the sunset. Eventually they were able to bathe him and bought him a fluffy pillow so he could spend his nights inside.

They'd skirted around the subject of what their forever looked like. Madison knew Ned would have to go back to Coronado soon, and that was going to be a real test of their relationship. He wanted her to move back with him. She wanted to stay in Florida. The issue remained unresolved. They still had a few days before he'd be returning to sort it out. She also knew he was wrapping his head around decisions he might have to make, since it wasn't his plan to remain in the Navy as a career.

Madison's mother got her little place put back together, had it completely repainted and went on an entertainment spree with her old friends. She explained that her mother often went through these swings. One moment reclusive, painting, reading, or gardening, and the next minute, she was having parties. Up until tonight, her mother had kept her distance.

One such party was planned for this evening, and her mother wanted them to come. It was a special invitation. Madison knew Ned was a little nervous about it.

She bought him a new shirt, a beautiful turquoise blue with pictures of starfish, seafoam and sand. His tanned skin and dark features made him look stunning in it.

"I'm still going to wear khakis and flip flops."

"As will most of the rest of the crowd."

Madison wore a light yellow dress with a low neck-line, perfect for displaying the mermaid pendant. She was going to braid her hair, but Ned insisted she wear it down and free. As was their custom, he placed the pendant around her neck and kissed her shoulders.

"She's not going to pepper me with questions, is she?"

Madison looked back at him through the mirror they were standing in front of. "Shouldn't she?"

"What kinds of questions?"

"The usual kinds of questions a mother will want to ask someone involved with her daughter."

He frowned.

She turned, wrapping her arms around him. "Just be yourself, Ned."

When they arrived, they could hear the party going in full force. Her mother had strung party lights around the backyard. There were five golf carts crammed into her driveway, plus a couple of bicycles. Ned parked in the alleyway, and as they walked to the front door, another golf cart arrived with four more partygoers, all grey-haired friends of her mothers, who greeted them warmly and then danced into the house.

"Honestly, Madison, these guys act like they're on college break," he said, following behind.

"Some of them came here on Spring Break and

never left!" She laughed at his puzzled expression.

"Will Noonan be here?"

"I'm guessing he will, but I didn't see his truck out front."

Inside, the place was festively decorated. The sliding glass door to the beach was wide open and half the partygoers were outside dancing to saxophone music.

"I'll introduce you to him later. He used to play with some really big bands in New Orleans and toured the world. Fascinating man," she told Ned.

"One of your mother's boyfriends?" he asked.

"Oh, I'm sure. Most of them are."

"How did you handle that growing up? I could never see my parents—"

"What's wrong?"

Ned pointed across the patio at several people drinking cocktails and laughing.

"I'm sorry. What are you looking at, Ned?"

"That's my mother!"

"No way. Which one?"

"Can't you tell?" he said exasperated. "The only one wearing a dark color. The lady in the navy dress wearing pearls."

The woman he described was standing right next to her mother, and the two were chatting, which surprised her most of all. Her mother was gracious, vivacious, and was wearing one of her brightest kaftans adorned with a shell necklace. She was telling some kind of story, her arms flying about her head. She made Ned's mother laugh. The two of them were having the same light pink cocktail drink.

"Ned, I didn't know anything about this," she whispered.

"Hello, kiddos!" A familiar voice came behind them. Noonan was clean shaven, had gotten a haircut, and once again had washed his patch.

Ned grabbed him by the collar. "Did you have a hand in this? You invited my mother to come talk to my father's ex-girlfriend?"

Madison was concerned he'd start making a scene. "Ned, stop it. You're going to embarrass me."

"Madison, this is not okay. You can't go playing with people's pasts like that, their deep-seated feelings. Just invite everyone to a party and ask them to mingle. This isn't a petri dish, you know."

"I invited her," said Noonan, recovering from the manhandling.

"And I accepted. I wanted to come," said his mother.

Ned turned to face her. "Are you okay with this? Do you know who she is?" he said pointing at Madison's mother standing at her side. People began to stare and even the music stopped.

Madison's eyes filled with tears. Ned looked like a

cornered bull. She felt so sorry for him. She brushed the tears from her cheeks and scolded Noonan.

"You should have told me. I could have prepared him."

"Why?" said her mother, her forehead furled, one hand on her hip. "He's a big boy. She's a grown woman. Why does she have to get permission from him to do anything? Noonan was just being nice, Ned. He paid her way."

"Mother?"

"I didn't realize it would upset you so, or I wouldn't have come." She was close to tears.

Noonan had to remind him, "Hug your mother, Ned."

"Oh, God," he muttered, holding her tight. "I'm sorry you got put in this position."

She looked confused, her arms flapping around his back before she finally hugged him back.

"Wait a minute." Madison's mother spoke up.

Ned dropped his arms and stepped away.

"You take a lot of liberty, Ned. This is *my* party. Noonan asked me, and I told him he could invite her. We both thought it was about time she was included. She has a family here, friends if she wants it, and the rest of her life to spend however she pleases. Are you even a part of the human race?"

Madison tried to pull her mother off, but she

wasn't having any of it.

"Let me finish, Maddie. He's made the scene, not me. He gets to live with it."

"He's trying to protect me," Mrs. Silver said. "That's all. He's just trying to protect me."

Ned stormed out of the house.

Madison looked between her mother and his mother, unsure what to do. "I'm sorry, sweetheart," his mother said to her. "I didn't realize he'd be so angry." She touched the pendant. "Look, Amberly, she's wearing Jake's pendant."

"As she should," said her mother.

The crowd started talking again, and someone put on music. Noonan stood still, looking like a fifth wheel. He finally shrugged and said, "All I wanted to do was surprise him. I never intended this to happen."

"It's okay, Noonan. We know. It's not you." Madison addressed Mrs. Silver. "Well, I'm glad you're here. We're all so happy you came to see our little piece of paradise. I've wanted to meet you." They clasped hands.

Her mother barked at Noonan. "Go get this girl a drink, please."

"Yes, ma'am." He departed on his mission.

Her mother began slowly. "So I have a theory, maybe a confession to make. My theory is that Madison is the real mermaid. Margaret, you might think me crazy, but Jake never should have been wearing that thing. It belongs on a woman's body. He never offered it to me, either. It never was for me or for you. It was for her."

Mrs. Silver's face was streaked in tears.

Her mom put her arm around Margaret Silver. "Come on, he was the sonofabitch we both loved for a time," she started. "You more than me. But let's be totally transparent here. He was a major handful. I loved him. But he knew I wouldn't put up with him. He knew it wouldn't last and I didn't have to say a thing. He knew you were the only one who could love him that much. He made the right decision. And I think, in that man's heart, he wanted us all to be here, together. This necklace brought Ned here. He brought back a little piece of Jake too."

Madison watched the two women walk away, holding hands, talking like two long-lost friends. Noonan handed her the drink that was ordered, but Madison had a hole in her heart the size of the State of California. Now she had to face one more challenge. What she'd do with the rest of her life if Ned left her behind, just like his dad left.

Except Madison was sure she had enough love for him. But she wasn't going to beg.

She didn't want to follow Ned, either, so set her drink down and walked through the patio and out toward the shore. The sky was orange. The surf was light greenish blue. Large puffy clouds caught purples and yellows as the sun met the horizon. She'd always told herself the beach could heal anything. It was the balm that would soothe anybody's soul, no matter what.

She inhaled, hoping that she could bring it all in and wash away all her sadness. She did it again, waited, and then let her breath out. Then she heard his voice behind her.

"Maddie, I'm a complete fool."

She didn't turn, in case her mind was playing tricks on her.

"Sweetheart, can you forgive me?"

It was Ned. She turned, letting him see her tears, not being afraid to let him see that she didn't want to lose him.

"You have to make up your mind, Ned, which way you want to go. You once told me I had to let a quiet man come in and rock my world, and I did. I tried it, and you were right. It's what I'd always wanted. But—"

She sniffled. It was a really ugly sniffle she had to wipe on her dress, but she didn't care.

She looked back at him and saw his tears.

"You're a good man. Probably the best man I've ever met. But you've got to stop saving people who don't want to be saved."

He blinked, not sure what he'd heard.

"You have to trust too. Like you asked me to trust. You have to let me love you back. I don't need saving, Ned. As long as I've got you, everything is perfect. Your mother made her choices. Now you've got to make yours. Ours, Ned. Are we going to live for this, today, or are we going to live in the past?"

He stepped to her, slipping his arm around her waist. She pressed her cheek against his, stepping up on tiptoes. Then he held her face in his hands, bent down, and kissed her.

"Today. It's all about today, Madison. No more ghosts or regrets. From now on. I'm not going anywhere."

She laughed. "You better not, or I'll have to kill you."

They heard the patio break out in cheers and clapping. They both turned their backs to their audience.

"Oh God, we have to go back and face them?" he mumbled, his arm around her shoulder.

She laughed, "I am. Are you?"

"Abso-fuckin'-lutely!"

Did you enjoy Treasure Island SEAL, Book 3 of my Sunset SEALs series? If so, won't you leave a review? Recommend this book on BookBub or GoodReads? Share a post about it?

Stay tuned for the next in this beautiful series:
Escape To Sunset,
Which is on pre order right now!

If you want to delve into the very beginning, don't forget Books 1 and 2 in Sunset SEALs:
SEALed At Sunset
Second Chance SEAL

And won't you join the family, following along with these other series:
SEAL Brotherhood (now in KU)
Bad Boys of SEAL Team 3
Band of Bachelors (now in KU)
Bone Frog Brotherhood

And for you audio fans, all of Sharon's books are performed by her superstar narrator, J.D. Hart of Nashville, Tennessee, and he sings too!
You can find all her listings on Audible.com.

ABOUT THE AUTHOR

 NYT and USA Today best-selling author Sharon Hamilton's award-winning Navy SEAL Brotherhood series have been a fan favorite from the day the first one was released. They've earned her the coveted Amazon author ranking of #1 in Romantic Suspense, Military Romance and Contemporary Romance categories, as well as in Gothic Romance for her Vampires of Tuscany and Guardian Angels. Her characters follow a sometimes rocky road to redemption through passion and true love.

Now that he's out of the Navy, Sharon can share with her readers that her son spent a decade as a Navy SEAL, and he's the inspiration for her books.

Her Golden Vampires of Tuscany are not like any vamps you've read about before, since they don't go to ground and can walk around in the full light of the sun.

Her Guardian Angels struggle with the human charges they are sent to save, often escaping their vanilla world of Heaven for the brief human one. You won't find any of these beings in any Sunday school class.

She lives in Sonoma County, California with her husband and her Doberman, Tucker. A lifelong organic gardener, when she's not writing, she's getting *verra verra* dirty in the mud, or wandering Farmers Markets looking for new Heirloom varieties of vegetables and flowers. She and her husband plan to cure their wanderlust (or make it worse) by traveling in their Diesel Class A Pusher, Romance Rider. Starting with this book, all her writing will be done on the road.

She loves hearing from her fans:
Sharonhamilton2001@gmail.com

Her website is:
sharonhamiltonauthor.com

Find out more about Sharon, her upcoming releases, appearances and news when you sign up for Sharon's newsletter.

Facebook:
facebook.com/SharonHamiltonAuthor

Twitter:
twitter.com/sharonlhamilton

Pinterest:
pinterest.com/AuthorSharonH

Amazon:
amazon.com/Sharon-Hamilton/e/B004FQQMAC

BookBub:
bookbub.com/authors/sharon-hamilton

Youtube:

youtube.com/channel/UCDInkxXFpXp_4Vnq08ZxMBQ

Soundcloud:

soundcloud.com/sharon-hamilton-1

Sharon Hamilton's Rockin' Romance Readers:

facebook.com/groups/sealteamromance

Sharon Hamilton's Goodreads Group:

goodreads.com/group/show/199125-sharon-hamilton-readers-group

Visit Sharon's Online Store:

sharon-hamilton-author.myshopify.com

Join Sharon's Review Teams:

eBook Reviews:

sharonhamiltonassistant@gmail.com

Audio Reviews:

sharonhamiltonassistant@gmail.com

Life is one fool thing after another.
Love is two fool things after each other.

REVIEWS

PRAISE FOR THE
GOLDEN VAMPIRES OF TUSCANY SERIES

"Well to say the least I was thoroughly surprise. I have read many Vampire books, from Ann Rice to Kym Grosso and few other Authors, so yes I do like Vampires, not the super scary ones from the old days, but the new ones are far more interesting far more human than one can remember. I found Honeymoon Bite a totally engrossing book, I was not able to put it down, page after page I found delight, love, understanding, well that is until the bad bad Vamp started being really bad. But seeing someone love another person so much that they would do anything to protect them, well that had me going, then well there was more and for a while I thought it was the end of a beautiful love story that spanned not only time but, spanned Italy and California. Won't divulge how it ended, but I did shed a few tears after screaming but Sharon Hamilton did not let me down, she took me on amazing trip that I loved, look forward to reading another Vampire book of hers."

"An excellent paranormal romance that was exciting, romantic, entertaining and very satisfying to read. It had me anticipating what would happen next many times over, so much so I could not put it down and even finished it up in a day. The vampires in this book were different from your average vampire, but I enjoy different variations and changes to the same old stuff. It made for a more unpredictable read and more adventurous to explore! Vampire lovers, any paranormal readers and even those who love the romance genre will enjoy Honeymoon Bite."

"This is the first non-Seal book of this author's I have read and I loved it. There is a cast-like hierarchy in this vampire community with humans at the very bottom and Golden vampires at the top. Lionel is a dark vampire who are servants of the Goldens. Phoebe is a Golden who has not decided if she will remain human or accept the turning to become a vampire. Either way she and Lionel can never be together since it is forbidden.

I enjoyed this story and I am looking forward to the next installment."

"A hauntingly romantic read. Old love lost and new love found. Family, heart, intrigue and vampires. Grabbed my attention and couldn't put down. Would definitely recommend."

PRAISE FOR THE
SEAL BROTHERHOOD SERIES

"Fans of Navy SEAL romance, I found a new author to feed your addiction. Finely written and loaded delicious with moments, Sharon Hamilton's storytelling satisfies like a thick bar of chocolate." —Marliss Melton, bestselling author of the *Team Twelve* Navy SEALs series

"Sharon Hamilton does an EXCELLENT job of fitting all the characters into a brotherhood of SEALS that may not be real but sure makes you feel that you have entered the circle and security of their world. The stories intertwine with each book before...and each book after and THAT is what makes Sharon Hamilton's SEAL Brotherhood Series so very interesting. You won't want to put down ANY of her books and they will keep you reading into the night when you should be sleeping. Start with this book...and you will not want to stop until you've read the whole series and then...you will be waiting for Sharon to write the next one." (5 Star Review)

"Kyle and Christy explode all over the pages in this first book, *[Accidental SEAL]*, in a whole new series of SEALs. If the twist and turns don't get your heart jumping, then maybe the suspense will. This is a must read for those that are looking for love and adventure with a little sloppy love thrown in for good measure." (5 Star Review)

PRAISE FOR THE
BAD BOYS OF SEAL TEAM 3 SERIES

"I love reading this series! Once you start these books, you can hardly put them down. The mix of romance and suspense keeps you turning the pages one right after another! Can't wait until the next book!" (5 Star Review)

"I love all of Sharon's Seal books, but *[SEAL's Code]* may just be her best to date. Danny and Luci's journey is filled with a wonderful insight into the Native American life. It is a love story that will fill you with warmth and contentment. You will enjoy Danny's journey to become a SEAL and his reasons for it. Good job Sharon!" (5 Star Review)

PRAISE FOR THE
BAND OF BACHELORS SERIES

"*[Lucas]* was the first book in the Band of Bachelors series and it was a phenomenal start. I loved how we got to see the other SEALs we all love and we got a look at Lucas and Marcy. They had an instant attraction, and their love was very intense. This book had it all, suspense, steamy romance, humor, everything you want in a riveting, outstanding read. I can't wait to read the next book in this series." (5 Star Review)

PRAISE FOR THE
TRUE BLUE SEALS SERIES

"Keep the tissues box nearby as you read *True Blue SEALs: Zak* by Sharon Hamilton. I imagine more than I wish to that the circumstances surrounding Zak and Amy are all too real for returning military personnel and their families. Ms. Hamilton has put us right in the middle of struggles and successes that these two high school sweethearts endure. I have read several of Sharon Hamilton's military romances but will say this is the most emotionally intense of the ones that I have read. This is a well-written, realistic story with authentic characters that will have you rooting for them and proud of those who serve to keep us safe. This is an author who writes amazing stories that you love and cry with the characters. Fans of Jessica Scott and Marliss Melton will want to add Sharon Hamilton to their list of realistic military romance writers." (5 Star Review)

"Dear FATHER IN HEAVEN,

If I may respectfully say so sometimes you are a strange God. Though you love all mankind,

It seems you have special predilections too.

You seem to love those men who can stand up alone who face impossible odds, Who challenge every bully and every tyrant ~

Those men who know the heat and loneliness of Calvary. Possibly you cherish men of this stamp because you recognize the mark of your only son in them.

Since this unique group of men known as the SEALs know Calvary and suffering, teach them now the mystery of the resurrection ~ that they are indestructible, that they will live forever because of their deep faith in you.

And when they do come to heaven, may I respectfully warn you, Dear Father, they also know how to celebrate. So please be ready for them when they insert under your pearly gates.

Bless them, their devoted Families and their Country on this glorious occasion.

We ask this through the merits of your Son, Christ Jesus the Lord, Amen."

By Reverend E.J. McMalhon S.J. LCDR, CHC, USN
Awards Ceremony SEAL Team One
1975 At NAB, Coronado

Made in the USA
Columbia, SC
04 July 2022